A
PROMISE

THE AGREEMENT II

by

R. D. SIMMONS

A PROMISE, THE AGREEMENT II

Cover Design by Shawn Fitzpatrick Design

Back Cover Photograph by John H Evans Jr. Photography

Indesign by Studio PaintedBlade, LLC

Tragedy to Triumph Books, Inc Fairview Heights, Il

ISBN 9780979158933

Acknowledgments

First, I would like to thank God for giving me strength and courage and for surrounding me with inspiring, high-quality people. You know who you are and thank you very much for putting up with me.

Of course, I must thank you for purchasing this book. I believe you will enjoy the story. Hopefully, I will see you at the end, when you visit my website and FaceBook page to ask to be my friend.

Thank you ahead of time.

Visit the Web site: **www.t2tbooks.com**

Facebook /theagreement123

Back at the Police Station

The three detectives are sitting in the room stunned by the story they just heard from the man in the house.

"Wait a minute sir, now you say that Fred was just trying to protect his family, right?" asked the head detective glancing at his coffee mug in his hand and then back at the man that was talking.

After another quick glance in his mug, he noticed that the mug was almost empty. He starts walking backwards towards the coffee maker and never taking his eyes off the man who is about to respond. As he reached for the coffee pot that was sitting on the coffee maker, he noticed it was empty too. "Wow. Before you go on with the story, I think it's time to take a break." The head detective said as he picked up the empty pot. "Can one of you get some more coffee brewing for me? I believe our man here has a lot more to say." He asked one of the rookie detectives to volunteer. "Do you still want to do all the talking? Because you two are still welcome to jump in anytime you wish."

Fred and Mrs. Johnson nods.

"Are we ready for our break detectives?" they both nodded. "Do any of you have to take a break to the restroom or something?"

"Sure, I can use a break." answered the man that was doing all the talking.

"Ok can you show him where the bathroom is?" asked the Head Detective to the rookie who didn't volunteer to make the coffee. Also, grab an officer to escort him back to this room because we must discuss some things and when we come back, begin where you ended." He added with a quick glance at the man of the house who nods to acknowledge that he understands.

As the detectives are walking out the room, the head detective puts one finger over his lips as he sees one of them getting ready to speak. His rule is to only discuss the case behind closed doors. When they arrived inside an office the anxious rookie name Detective Billips quickly discusses his concerns.

"I don't believe he is telling us everything." Detective Billips said.

"Well we will find out as soon as we get more evidence." responded the Chief Detective sitting down at his desk checking his cell phone Caller I.D. to see who called. "Okay, here is what I need each of you to do." he said as he put the cell phone down. "I need one of you to take this gun down to ballistics. I need another you to print up a form for them to sign and leave their prints. We need some leads and we got to get them anyway we can." He added taking turns and establishing eye contact with both of them. "Now I have to go call the hospital and check on the injured detective and then go and get the rest of that story."

The man in the house walked back into the interrogation room with an officer. Meanwhile, the other two suspects are sitting in the interrogation room thinking about the commotion that just took place at the home.

"Hey, just let me keep doing all the talking. I will fix this, alright." said the man that was in the house after the officers exited the interrogation room. "Now, where did I stop?"

The Beginning of the End

Ahhhh, Ahhhhhh, Ahhhh, screamed Mrs. Johnson as she runs back to her room. Fred drops the gun and runs out the front door and runs into someone with all black on and hair facial. He gets up and starts back running again not even looking at who he just ran into. The intruder stares at the person who was shot not even noticing the man at the door. Then the man at the door walks in holding a gun. The intruder reaches for the gun that Fred dropped on the floor. "Watch it Mr. Johnson, you don't want to do that."

"Wait a minute, how did you know my name." Mr. Johnson narrowed his eyes to look harder. "Dr. Cashion is that you?"

"That's right, it sure is and I came from prison and came right to your house. To see why u couldn't keep our agreement! Why you never checked on me in prison and why were you nowhere to be found when I went to court."

"Well, you know how it is." responded Mr. Johnson shrugging his shoulders.

"Well whatever, I got who I really wanted. That was Ted, right and was that the son you said you were going to adopt that ran out of here?"

Mr. Johnson nods.

"Why was Ted over here? And why did your son run and not stay here with you?"

"Apparently he is scared; he just shot him." Mr. Johnson replied pointing his thumb at the injured person on the floor.

"Oh he did. Hell man, let me make sure he is dead."

The doctor walks over to Ted who was lying behind some boxes to check his pulse and the wound. "Aye it looks like someone was about to move." He said walking over boxes to get to Ted lying on the floor.

"Wow. Yep he's a gonna. That's what he gets for double crossing me." Silence as he moves Ted shirt up. "He has only been shot once." Dr. Cashion said showing Mr. Johnson where he was shot.

"I wonder which one of you shot him. I did only hear one shot go off." said Mr. Johnson as he walks over to pick up the gun Fred had in his hand.

"Oh! So you shot him. I thought Fred shot him." said Mr. Johnson as he looks down the barrel and sees no clip. "It's not loaded, he added."

"Okay, I must have shot him. You know I was coming here to find you to ask you why you didn't keep your agreement. But when I got here I saw you fighting Ted and I was like, just the person I need to see. I pulled out my gun and shot him after he slammed you to the floor. I was going to shot him again but that boy ran into me... There was a pause when a sudden thought came to the doctor's head. "That's it! Hey, I need you to do me a favor."

"What, you want a favor done and you just came to my house with a gun? Who was that gun for if Ted wasn't here. The nerve!"

"Now you know I am not going to shot you. I really wanted to just scare you for not being a man of your word after we made the agreement for me to do that for your son."

"You know, I think Mr. Smith put a hex on us. All this time and this is still hunting us. A brief pause as they both look at each other and nod. "Alright, hurry it up and tell me, because I am sure someone called the police by now." Mr. Johnson said without an expression.

"Okay, you are right. Here is what I'm going to need you to do."

"Dajavoo." Mr. Johnson thought as he listened to Dr. Cashion's plan.

"Mr. Johnson just say Fred shot him. He will never get no time being a juvenile."

"Yeah, I can say that this guy ran in on my family, so my boy shot him. Now get out of here before the police come. I am cool with that. So get out of here." Mr. Johnson brushes his idea off and walking in front of him to guide him out the door.

"Okay, let's shake on it like you made me do with your other son."

They shook hands.

"Okay, looks like it's another agreement."

I owe it to you again anyway for getting rid of this man for me. This time I didn't have to pay you anything. But, it's an agreement." Mr. Johnson said at the release of the hand shake.

"No, no, no." Dr. Cashion reached for his hand again. "We are not going to call it an agreement this time. "Let's called it a promise and maybe the hex will leave. Let's say it's a promise." He said looking intensely in his eyes.

"Alright, well it's a promise."

They both shook hands again but this time they both had their free hand behind their back.

Dr. Cashion exchanged the other gun and dashes out the door. "You don't mine do you? Aye get Fred to put his finger prints on this. The doctor said wiping his prints off the gun and hands it to Mr. Johnson with the cloth. "I will be in touch." He hollered before turning his back and running to his car and driving away.

Minutes later the police arrived with the EMT workers.

"Sir are you the only one here?" asked the first arriving detective Detective Billips as soon as he sees Mr. Johnson walks in from the back.

"Heee, heee." cried Mrs. Johnson in the bedroom in the back.

"What's that noise in the back room there? It sounds like I hear someone crying."

"Yes' the Misses back there." responded Mr. Johnson looking in the direction where the noise is coming from.

"Oh, is that right?" He pointed to another arriving officer to go get Mrs. Johnson.

"Did you shoot the man?" The officer asked Mr. Johnson while the EMT is checking for Ted's pulse.

The EMT put the sheet over Ted's face and carries him away.

"Wow. The officer said unexpectedly. "We have a homicide. Where is the gun that shot him?" The officer noticed Mr. Johnson pointing in the hallway.

"So again, who shot him?" he asked again walking towards where the gun lies as Mr. Johnson moves to the side.

"My son, he was trying to protect us."

The police looked at the gun and noticed it looks as if it's been used a lot.

"Sir is this gun registered?" He asked turning the gun sideways to see the serial number.

"Uh, Uh, Uh, I don't know, where it came from it's not mines. I guess he found that gun?"

"What!" the officer blurted as he knew that Mr. Johnson was pulling his leg. "Well, we can check the serial number and the ballistics and see who this gun belongs too.--------"Where is he?"

"Who?"--------"My son?"

The officer nods.

"He ran out the door?" Mr. Johnson said as he points at the front door.

"Go see if you can find him?" He asked the closest police officer standing beside him.

"What does he look like?" asked the officer taking out his small note pad that was in his shirt pocket.

"He is about 5'4" with a red shirt on."

"His name is what again?" asked the officer while scribbling notes on his pad.

"Fred, the name is Fred Smith." said Mr. Johnson.

"Little Fred?" the officer continued stretching his arm down and opening his hand in front of him to exhibit a short person.

Mr. Johnson nods.

"I met him before. Him and his Grandma rode in my car one day. I'll see if I can find him." he dashes out the door and gets on his radio. "Officer, be on the lookout for a, a, he stutters as he sees someone peaking out of a red Buick with a red shirt on. "Strike that officers." He walks slowly over there not sure if Fred is armed; he stoops down behind the car. "Fred, this is Officer Perkins can you get out with your hands up for me? Silence as there was no response. Fred I see you in the car and everything is going to be alright, okay."

"I didn't mean to shoot him!" Fred cried out.

"I know. Just come out. It's me Officer Perkins. You remember me right." Silence as officer waves off the bystanders coming out to see what's going on.

"Look, you taking care of your family will be considered and you will be release very soon. We just need for you to tell them that back at the station. So come on, everything will be alright. You can trust me, Hell, I remember you when you were a little younger, you hopped in my squad car and you were fascinated. You were looking around waving at people. You seem harmless. So come on out and we will take care of this together."

Fred opens the door and slowly climbs out.

"Fred put your hands up where I can see them." asked the officer with his hand on his side.

Fred comes out very slowly and he raised his hands up in the air like the officer asked him.

"Fred I have to put these on, because I don't want to lose you." He said putting the handcuffs on one arm then the other one.

Fred and Officer Perkins walk to the door.

"I found our man." said Officer Perkins when he got to the door.

"Come on let's go down to the station, so we can be done with this soon." said Detective Billips. It looks as if this can be justified real soon, because he shared that he was just trying to protect his family like Mr. Johnson said."

"Okay, but Fred, Fred where did you find this gun?" asked Detective Billips.

Fred looked at the gun and motions his head in disagreement. "That's not the gun." He added with the motion.

"Okay, he may be a little disarranged from all the excitement." Mr. Johnson said quickly.

"Miss, do you remember this gun?" he asked Mrs. Johnson and then noticed the cut on her hand.

"No I don't like guns so I never paid it a lot of attention, but I believe our gun was never that old looking." She replied with narrow eyes and head movement.

"But you are not sure?" he asked again as he moves the gun to get her to look again.

"No, I am afraid not."

"Okay, so tell me, what happened to your hand?"

She looks down at her hand. "Oh this, I just cut it on a glass when I was packing."

"Okay. It seems as if it's a good job with the wrap. You may want to get one of the EMT's to check it out for you." he said in disbelief. "Well let's all go back down to the station to get this resolved."

"I will take them in my car." said Officers Perkins detaching his keys away from his belt buckle. "Hey by the way, did we ever find out what happened to Detective Mac, and is he going to be alright? He continued holding Fred's arm to escort him out of the door with Mr. Johnson.

The officer nods his head.

"Did somebody catch a suspect?"

"No not yet, at first I thought it was that doctor who got convicted and they just released. But he wasn't released from prison at the time the shooting happened. But anyway, I was told that he was going to be alright. I will see you back at the station in a minute."

"Good because he is a good detective. See yah."

"That may be why someone wants him killed." He mumbled.

Officer Perkins glances at the officer who was talking and nods his head in agreement. "Man, I wonder who shot him." He says to himself as he puts Fred in the back seat. Fred thinks of that day with his grandma. Unfortunately, this time it is for real. He thought to himself while the officer opens the passenger's door for Mr. Johnson who is wearing a suspicious smile. He then opens up the back seat driver door for Mrs. Johnson.

"Hey, do you think you know who's behind the shooting? Because I don't like that look on your face," asked the Officer Perkins noticing Mr. Johnson's sarcastic look.

"No. No, Officer. I am thinking of something else." Said Mr. Johnson wondering if Dr. Cashion was involved with the shooting of the detective too.

When the Doctor Met Brent the Hit Man

It's in the afternoon and the prison guards are letting out the prisoners for some afternoon stretching. The doctor walks to a bench and sits down with a newspaper in his hand. As he opens the paper, suddenly a prisoner named Brent walks towards him.

"Hey Doctor, what's up?" asked Brent as he sees the doctor reading a newspaper.

"Not this confinement." he responded putting down the paper to show that Brent has his attention.

"Yeah, I feel you. But you know my days are numbered."

"Yes I realize that, but you do remember our promise right?"

Brent nods.

"Are you going to keep it?"

"Yeah, it's not every day you find a doctor who knows what to tell a doctor to help my mother."

"Speaking of her, how is she doing?" asked the doctor looking concerned.

"Man she is doing a hundred percent better. She has never been so proud of me. I thought I was a disappointment to her. Isn't that awkward, I had to go to prison to find the right help for my mother."

"Brent you can find help anywhere, now just deal with your promise and how are you going to pull it off." The doctor said pinching his lips.

"Doc, don't worry about that, I got everything set up."

"Here, stand up and put your right hand up to give me your word."

Brent hesitated as he looked at the doctor who wasn't smiling. "Man alright." He stands."

"Ha ha ha." He chuckles. "Brent, why are you in here again?" He asked.

"Man, if I wouldn't have met the rich guy Ted hooked me up with some rich guy that Ted hook me up with, I never would have got caught with all that money. When the cops pulled me over for speeding, I couldn't think of a good lie to tell them, on why I had so much money on me. So I just told them I was going to buy a house. They later found a warrant for my arrest. So when I went to court, the judge decided to keep me in prison in case I was getting ready to make a drug deal. Ain't that some bull?"

"Oh, I guess let's hear the promise."

Brent slops his back. "I promise to take care of the detective." he said softly.

"Good."

"When do you think you will be out of here anyway?" asked Brent quickly putting his hand down before someone sees him.

"Well, my lawyer told me that they are looking at some things to overturn the case of Detective Mac trying to set me up. If what they say is true, I will be out of here in about four more months." he said putting up four fingers.

"Cool, I will have that waiting on you alright."

The doctor looks puzzled.

"You know?"

"Oh yeah, I will need that."

"Alright Doc, I got to go and call my mother, she should be out of church now." Brent said while giving the doctor a hand shake.

Brent and his Mother Mrs. Byrd

Brent walks toward a pay phone outside. He waits as someone is using the phone. The man is apparently talking to his girlfriend.

"Baby, I know you have to go back to work but my time is not up." said the prisoner into the phone.

Brent looks at his watch as he over hears his conversation and confirms prisoner's statement.

"Besides, Curt knows me from coming in his store to see you, so he should be alright if you are a little late. Just tell him you were talking to me."

Brent checks his watch again. "A man! Phone check!" He yelled.

The prisoner looks up at him. "Man hold on." He replied narrowing his eyes.

"You know when I get out of here we going to get married, right." said the prisoner when he returned back to the phone. "What you mean you don't want to marry me." He said turning his back to get more privacy. "What you mean you want to break up with me, you know I need you. How come you telling me this and I am all in prison and stuff._____ "What? You are not going to accept my calls anymore too? Alright, bitch. I will be taking care of you and him when I get out." He said angrily quickly glancing at Brent to see if he's listening to his conversation then he puts his head down and lets out a breath.

19

At that second Brent walks toward the phone and pushes down the click on the phone.

"What the!" He stops his actions as he notices a guard staring at him with a raised brow.

"Look your time is up!" Brent said pointing at the stop clock above the phone.

"Man, whatever. Here!" He drops the phone before Brent grabs it and smirks.

Brent picks up the phone as he stares at the prisoner momentarily. He then dials zero for the operator and asked her to call his mother.

"Hello." answered the operator.

"I would like to make a collect call."

As he explained the information with the operator he held the phone to his ear with one arm up against the hard steel cover over the phone.

"This is the operator. I have a collect call from a Brent Byrd inmate. Will you accept?"

"Yes," responded Brent's mother softly.

"Hey mom, you sound like you are not happy to hear from me."

"Son, I am but I am tired of paying this high phone bill."

"I know mother I will be out soon."

"I heard that before." She replied slanting her lips.

"No mother it's serious this time."

"OK, when will that doctor be out, dough?"

"Ain't no telling. But he said he will be out soon as well."

"Good, because I want to thank him personally. How did you get him to do that for you anyway?"

"Mom don't worry about that, what's important is that you are alright."

"Come on, don't give me that, you had to promise him something."

"Mom." Brent responded letting out a breath.

"Okay Brent, just let him know that if he ever need anything that I will be her for him."

"Alright, Mom you used all my time, talking about the doctor, what about me."

"Boy you are grown, stop whining like a baby. But anyway, you are right your time is up, because your brother just walked in. So, when will you be out of there?"

In a couple of weeks. He softly said feeling sad because his brother gets all the attention.

"Okay, I got your room ready."

"Thank you mom, and………..

"Son, I am sorry. I got to go finish cooking for your brother please don't try to start another conversation. I sent you some stamp money, say it in a letter. Alright." Ms. Byrd added cutting him off.

"Alright mom."

"The only reason I accepted your phone calls when you first went into prison was because I…. Never mind. But I knew you weren't going to be in there long."

"Yeah, it was a good thing that I listened to you that day."

"Alright son you be good, so I can see you soon, goodbye. I got to go. Goodbye."

Brent hears a click before he can respond.

The First Time Brent went to Jail

Brent grew up in the South side of the ghetto. He has only one older brother who is a manager at a grocery store off of King's street. However, his mother treats his brother like he's an only son. You see Brent started hanging out with the wrong crowd a long-time ago. He tried to get back on track but he never could. He was in and out of jobs and he even tried to work at his brother's grocery store but was asked to leave after some accusations of selling drugs at the store. He was always jealous of his brother and he became angrier when he assumed that his brother was dating a married clerk. But what put the icing on the cake about his brother is when this married woman made head cashier. To this day, he wonders if his brother had something to do with her husband's death.

Well anyway after his firing, Brent really couldn't find a stable job so he decided to sell drugs in the street. While selling drugs in the street, he runs into Ted one day. At the time, Ted was sorrowful because his mother was being evicted. So Ted joined the drug gang and everybody liked him because he was dependable and people liked his services. Brent knew that he couldn't trust anyone but he really wanted to start trusting Ted were liked his persona. Brent thought that the only person he can really trust was his mother. Too bad his mother couldn't trust him.

Every day, he tries to impress his mother with gifts and money. Although, she accepted a lot of the small gifts, she assumed that he was working hustles but when Brent started giving his mom big gifts, she started getting suspicious. Later, she realized that Brent was doing exactly what she expected. When she found out that he was selling drugs, she grew worried so much so that she called the police on him when she found out that the police were looking for him for questioning. The police caught him and Ted. Ted was release. Anyway, Mrs. Byrd felt bad about what she did then she realized that her son may be safer in jail. She prayed for him daily.

"Heavenly father, please take care of my son. You said in your word that "you will never leave us or forsake us." I know your word is true and therefore I will wait for this to come to pass. Thank you Jesus."

"Ring, ring, ring." The sound of a telephone rings interrupting her prayer.

"Hello Mama, they are trying to put this on me."

"Did you do anything?"

"Hell nooo."

"Boy watch your mouth, I just got through praying for you."

"Oh, my bad, but this shit ain't right. Oops sorry again. Mamma what can I do?"

"Son just listen to the police because they will steer you in the right direction."

"Yell right, they want me to work out a plea to squeal on this person I know."

"Well, you think that person will do the same for you?" She responded looking up and seeing her favorite son Curtis walk into the house."

"I don't know. But I am not a squeal."

"OK, be not a squeal while being in jail for a long time and the other person out here free as a bird."

"But mama…………"

"But honey I got to go. Your brother just came in and he looks upset. So I will talk to you later, goodbye."

"Well, ……."

"Click hmmmmmmmmmmm." The phone says suddenly.

He takes a seat and thinks about what his mother just said about being locked up for a long time because he didn't want to squeal. Before the day ended, he made up his mind to take the plea. He met his attorney and the detective to talk about the plea.

"Hello, Mr. Brent Byrd. My name is Detective Mac, and this is your attorney, Attorney George Greene. They give each other a nod and a hand shake. I found that your prints match another case and now I'm going to let your attorney discuss with you what we found and how you can get a lighter sentence if you help us get someone, alright.

"Well, before we go any further why don't we let you discuss some of the details with your attorney before me and the head detective of the case come back."

Detective Mac leaves the room but before he leaves, he thought to get the coffee brewing. He knows that the head detective likes coffee during his sessions and he is always trying to make a good impression. He left the room and allowed the two to discuss the perimeters of his decision.

Moments later the detective walks in with the head detective.

"You got the coffee ready." said the head detective excited and walking towards the coffee pot. "You are always thinking…. I like that in you." He said to Detective Mac as he grabs the pitcher and pours the coffee in his personal mug he always carries.

"He will take the plea." said his attorney.

"Are you promising us you will tell us everything?"

"Yeah." Brent said with no expression.

"So you understand everything the detective shared with you."

He nods. "Yeah, I am cool." He added looking down.

"Okay, so what's your plea?"

"He will share everything he knows for probation." The attorney said firmly.

"Good. Well, Attorney Green that will be all."

Detective Mac walks him out the room.

He returns with the head detective, Brent asked him a question as the head detective reviews some paperwork.

"Aye man aren't you the one caught my boy Ted when you caught me.

"Yeah." He said looking down.

"Why did you let him go?"

"What do you mean why we let him go, we weren't looking for him." He said quickly looking up then back at what the detective was doing.

"Oh. But you didn't catch nothing on him?" he asked in a curious tone.

"No, he was clean." Detective Mac said as he remembers that day when he asked Ted to act as his informer.

"Anyway, what do you know?" The head detective cuts in to get to the point.

Brent told them everything he knew and he was released for probation. And the cops put out an APB on the person he told on. Brent hopes and pray that word never gets out about what he did.

Opps, I Made a Mistake

The Johnson's are just finishing the questioning with the detectives about the shooting that went on at the house.

"Well it looks as if this shooting was probable cause. You say he was just trying to protect the family right."

Mr. Johnson nods his head in agreement.

"Well okay if you all don't mind, I am going to need you two to sign this form. It's just saying that we discussed the case and agree to the circumstances of the case pending further investigation."

Mr. Johnson extends his hand to grab the form and hands the other sheet to Mrs. Johnson to sign. When Mrs. Johnson signs it, she realized that she messed up.

"Oops, I messed up. Can I have another form?" she asked Detective Billips.

"You messed up signing your name. **Felicia** Hum……. What were you getting ready to spell?" He asked staring hard at the form.

"Oh, I was getting ready to sign my maiden name."

"Your maiden name doesn't starts with an H!" he said angrily and he starts wondering if she got married again while he was away. *"But how did she do that? I wasn't gone that long."* He thought.

"Ma'am, just rewrite your whole name under the name you mess up on. That should be fine." Detective Billips said.

Mrs. Johnson rewrites her name nervously shaking the pin.

"Okay, I guess that says Felicia Johnson." responded Detective Billips looking at the scribbled signature.

"Detectives, can I see you for a minute?" asked a forensic officer who just opened the door a crack.

The detective excused himself and walked in unison out the door, closing it behind them.

Mr. Johnson gives Mrs. Johnson a hard stare.

Felicia puts her head down.

"Again, why did you almost write another name on the form?"

"It was just a mistake."

"Lady I know a mistake when I see one!"

"You know, I thought this was the end of this chapter in my life. Why did our son have that bad heart?"

"Well, I don't think it was because he had a bad heart but what we had Dr. Cashion do for us."

She nods.

"Now let's get back on the subject." He said returning his hard stare.

"What?"

"You know what? Your maiden name was Currie. How did you get that mixed up with Hum?"

"I was thinking about something else, please stop this."

"What!" Mr. Johnson said disgusted.

Mrs. Johnson looks away in silence.

Not a moment too soon, two detectives come back in furious.

"Hey where did you say you got that gun from?" asked the first detective.

"I, I found it." Mr. Johnson responded nervously.

"Well we checked the ballistics and it looks as if that was the same gun that was used to shoot a detective."

"When was this?"

"Earlier today."

That must have been where the ambulances were going that Ted said he heard when I just cut my hand. Mrs. Johnson thought glazing at the cut.

"I hope you got a great alibi." The detective said with no expression.

"Since the gun is not registered and we got that evidence we are going to have to keep you longer. Mrs. Johnson and Fred can go home for now."

"I will be talking to you later." Said Mr. Johnson as Mrs. Johnson gets up to leave the house.

She nods with a slight smile.

"For how much longer?" Mr. Johnson asked watching Mrs. Johnson and Fred exit the room.

"We just got some more questioning and wait until we contact Detective Mac to see if there is a connection."

Mr. Johnson gives the detectives a stare without an expression as he hopes that the detective doesn't remember running into him or the connection.

Mrs. Johnson grabs Fred and Officer Perkins takes them back home.

"Now sir can you prove where you were on Wednesday February 11 of this year?" asked the detective.

"Yeah, I was in New York."

"Where at?"

"Ok, ok, I was in New York, New York.

"Sir, what did you go there for?"

"Sir, I just went on business."

"Is that why you shot Mr. Humphrey because he was with your wife when you came back home."

"Who? Is that that man's last name?"

"Yeah that was his last name, his first name was Teddy."

"Yeah, I know that but." He paused. "Never mind "

"Yeah? But, I thought you said he was an intruder and you never met him before. So how did you know his first name?"

"I just heard you all say his name." Mr. Johnson responded quickly.

Detective Billips looks at Mr. Johnson with a raised brow.

"Hey Detective, we got Detective Mac on the phone." The voice of the secretary came through the phone speakers.

"Good, maybe we can get to the bottom of this." responded Detective Billips.

Mr. Johnson stares off.

"Hello, Detective Mac. How are you?"

"Fine, but I can be doing better once I get out of here and find out who did this to me. What's up?"

"Well speaking of which, we found the gun that bullet came from?"

"Oh yeah, do you have the perpetrator."

"Perhaps, if this guys alibi don't fly."

"What thug did this to me?"

"Well actually, this guy is a professional."

"Wait, it's not that Doctor is it?"

"What Doctor?"

"Dr. Cashion, I had a feeling that that man was going to be after me for what I had done to him but he was still locked up when I got shot, right?"

"Yes, as far as I know, anyway this guy is no doctor. Do you know a Reginald Johnson?"

"Johnson, Johnson." He said twice trying to remember why that name rings a bell. "You know what? I think I remember a Johnson from Dr. Cashion's case. Pull up that case on my computer. I am sure a Johnson name will come up somewhere."

"Alright, what's your password?"

"My last name and badge number four, two and six."

"Got it."

"Alright, I will be talking to you later."

Detective Billips hangs up the phone and walks over to the secretary's desk. "Here, can you look this name and the cases for me?" he asked her standing over her shoulders while she is sitting at her desk.

The detective walks back to the room where Mr. Johnson is sitting with his head on the table.

"Well Mr. Johnson, the Detective couldn't remember you directly but he thinks he knows your name."

"Tell me, do you know a Dr. Cashion?"

"Yeah, he did work on my son."

"Who, Fred?"

33

"No, my deceased son."

"Oh, excuse me. Can I ask what happened?"

"That's another story, let's just stick to this."

"Well, you know what happened to Dr. Cashion?"

"Yeah, but he's out now."

"Yeah, talking about it was unconstitutional to set him up. I mean if the man was doing wrong, so be it. This system is messed up." The detective slanting his lips.

Mr. Johnson just looks expressionless.

"So are we still in touch with the doctor?"

"We are associated." He replies irritated. "Man can I leave?"

"No, not yet. As soon as you prove your whereabouts then we can go."

"Here." said Mr. Johnson reaching for his notepad to write the phone number down where he was that day.

"Excuse me." Said Detective Billips as he presses the secretary's code. "Can you call this number?" He recites the number to her and had her to repeat it.

He hangs up and gives Mr. Johnson a penetrating stare.

"Oh yeah, here you go." He hands him a state ID of a fake name. "I was going by that name when I was down there."

"What's this?" He gives the ID a penetrating stare. "Wow this is good." A brief moment of silence as he takes in the good work on the id. "Anyway Mr. Johnson sir, this is against the law. Is this the name you was going by." He asked pointing at the name on the license and showing it to him.

"I am not trying to be funny or nothing but your son was a donor recipient, right.'

Mr. Johnson nods his head.

"And you marked no on the donor objections."

Mr. Johnson nods again, this time irritated.

"Well, I will be back to talk to you some more soon."

Mr. Johnson grew even more irritated. "You know, I am not saying nothing else until I see a lawyer!" Mr. Johnson said while pushing away from the table and folding his arms. "How long you think you can keep me?"

"Well sir we can keep you as long as we are doing this investigation. We got you for at least 48 hours. Hell we could have kept your wife and your son, but we changed our minds. We felt they were clear and the boy been through a lot already."

"Yes, you only know half of what that boy been through."

"Yeah but look, I got to go and take care of this and I will see you later." said Detective Billips taking quick steps out of the door.

"Wait a minute, where are you going with my I.D.?"

"I have to confiscate this and make it a part of our records. Sit tight I will be back."

Man, I started not to come back home. He thought while staring at the detective walking out the door.

"Detective Billips," he yelled at the officer when he sees him coming out the door. "We got a hold of that person in New York and they said that he was there at that time. But they didn't know who he was but assumed that we were talking about this person. When we asked to describe him, she nailed it. She went as far as naming where his birth mark was. That was TMI. But she said that he was going by this name. The detective looked at a paper in his hand and compared the name with the drivers license he was carrying in his hand."

"Okay, looks like his alibi is good."

"Yeah anyway, they want to know where he was and for him to contact her right away. Here is her name and whereabouts." he continued handing him another piece of paper.

He takes the paper from the officer and walks back towards the interrogation room.

Mr. Johnson, looks as if it's your lucky day.

Mr. Johnson looks at the detective wondering if that was a sarcastic remark.

"Well we checked your whereabouts and it was true, you were in New York. So, I guess we have to release you."

"Good."

"Well make sure you don't skip town, because we may need to reach you again."

Mr. Johnson nods his head.

Where was Mr. Johnson

When Reggie Johnson was in Mexico, he started seeing someone else. He never told her that he was married but was in Mexico for some development projects. Anyway, Reggie and his new friend were very involved with each other but during the time he couldn't stop thinking about his wife at home. He stayed in Mexico until he thought it was safe to come back. But Reggie is such a business man he crack some business deals and wasn't able to come back when he heard that the doctor went to jail for what he did. So, Reggie had to fix the deal first and then he felt that it will be wise to come home afterwards.

However, Reggie and the lady he was involved with name is Samatha. Samatha got real close with Reggie the way Mrs. Johnson felt in love with him. They were intrigue on how he handled his business. At least Samantha thought so. Reggie was having a lot of fun and was thinking about making a change. He also wanted another son and knew if he stayed with his wife this wouldn't be possible. So, during his stay he had a lot of things racing in his head. He didn't know what to do. But he did miss his wife back home. Before he left he made love to his mistress one last time, then he told her that he has a wife back home in the north and that he was going back to be with her forever. She was crushed.

On the way home from the station, Mr. Johnson unfolds the paper the police gave to him. The paper read very, very urgent. He reads the number and remembers to himself that he already has that number locked in his phone.

"Oh, I got this number." He said to himself pressing speed dial on his cell phone.

When a young lady answers the phone, Mr. Johnson raised his voice.

"What's the matter with you? I told you it was over because I am married! Why are you trying to contact me."

"I am pregnant." She replied with a swallow.

"What!"

"I said, I am pregnant." she repeats firmly this time.

Mr. Johnson was speechless as Mr. Johnson thinks about his wife and what she will think. Almost immediately he starts thinking about what just happened at the police station in regards to Mrs. Johnson almost writing the wrong name down.

"Hello." said the person on the other end growing impatient with the silence.

"You know what? This is too much for me to handle right now. I will call you after nine months." He lets out some air. "You know we have to take a blood test." he suggested.

"What, I only…."

Before she can finish Mr. Johnson hangs up the phone and continue to drive home preparing to confront his wife.

Dear Reggie

When Mr. Johnson arrived home, he was anxious to tell Mrs. Johnson that he found out what name she was getting ready to write on that form. But, when he arrived, the house was empty.

"Damn it, you know it did look as if they were packing and getting ready to move when I came back here and got into it with Ted." He said to himself as he was walking through the house checking every room.

After he realized that no one was really there, he sat down in the corner. He then noticed a letter sticking on the refrigerator door. He gets up to get it.

"What's this?" He said to himself snatching the paper off the refrigerator.

He reads the letter to himself:

Dear Reggie, I am sorry but I closed this chapter in my life. You know you took me through a lot in the last chapter but this chapter I would rather be on my own. I am not interested in sending Fred through this as well. So we just packed our things and left to a destination that is a secret at this time. I will contact you when I am ready, why didn't you contact me when you left? Oh, I know why. I guess you were trying to fix what was going on at the time. You are always trying to fix things. Like you tried to fix our wedding. Well honey that backfired like everything else. You see I did get remarried or married, so I am no longer your wife. You didn't cross your t's and dot your i's. Our marriage contract was not signed by an ordained minister. So I did what I had to do. Please go on with your life. I want a new chapter in my life.

Luv, Felicia

Mr. Johnson balls the paper up furiously and throws it in the corner. "What is she doing? I did everything for her including paying for that damn wedding."

Mr. Johnson walks out and hops into the car to look for her. He checked everywhere, until he became hungry and needed a snack. He pulls over to a store that looks like it's about to close. While he was shopping for his items, he over hears a man and an older lady talking.

"Son, every since your boy got out, he has been eating me out of a house and a home."

"Well momma you are not going to eat me out of a store and a job."

"No, I will get only the things I need. But anyway you know I got a call earlier from a church member and she was talking about leaving town. My answering service went dead before she told me where and why. You know, that's one lady with a lot of money and a lot of problems coming with it. It kinda reminds me of one of those album covers when you and your brother was D. Jing. I think it read More Money More Problems. You know she had a lot of problems with her ex-husband trying to fix everything with his money. But I guess he couldn't fix death. But anyway, she did feel happier after she remarried or married that other man. But she sounds really upset on the answering service. I wonder why?" she stares off expressionless.

"Oh, you haven't heard." Her son responds with a quick thought to her head. He excused the cashier girl to the side to ring her out with his discount. Mr. Johnson comes and stands behind her.

"Heard what?"

"Well, an intruder tried to break-in and got shot and the intruder was Ted her new husband."

"How is her husband going to break in his own house?"

"Hey excuse me." Mr. Johnson said getting their attention. "But I think you all are talking about my wife."

"Oh,_____ Mr. Johnson????" she said curious and looking over her shoulders and staring at him while narrowing her eyes.

When Mr. Johnson nods, her knees get weak.

Mr. Johnson catches her. "Wow, you need to sit down." Her son grabs the chair that this lazy cashier sits on when she's at work.

"Here, she can sit here."

He puts the chair under her legs forcing her knees to bend down in the chair. Reggie doesn't even wait to make sure she is comfortable before he asked.

"Have you seen my wife?"

"Man, let her go. I am trying to make sure my mother is okay. No, I haven't seen your wife. Trish can you grab me a bucket so I can prop her legs on it." He asked one of the cashiers. "Momma,

41

are you okay?" Curt asked waving a magazine he just took off the counter.

He looks at Mr. Johnson and starts thinking about the last time, what happened years ago when a man came in the store about his wife.

"Hey, are you a ghost?" His mother asked opening her eyes repeatedly.

"No ma'am. I never was dead."

"So how did you come back to life?" she asked while **Trish** places the bucket by her legs.

"Here momma, put your legs on this bucket." Curtis says as he grabs a jacket that Trish keeps at work for when she gets cold. "You don't mind do you?" he asked Trish.

Trish motions her head to say no.

He folds the jacket up to add cushion and places it on top of the bucket. He then takes her legs and places them on top of her jacket.

"Well to answer your question, I never was dead."

Curtis stares off in deep thought, *he starts thinking about that time and how they never found his body.* "Oh, that's right they never found your body. That was big news around here when that happened."

"I should have known that you were up to something. Your wife told me that you were that type of person. What was your nick name again? Mr. Fix it, right?" said Ms. Byrd as she tights her face.

Mr. Johnson gives her a look with no expression. "Now again, have you seen my wife?" he asked.

"You still claiming her, huh?" Ms. Byrd said smacking her lips again and rolling her eyes.

"Ma'am, I know she is married, you don't have to beat around the bush on me!" Mr. Johnson changing his tone and growing angry.

"Alright, watch your tone, I am your elder."

"Sir, you are going to have to leave my store getting my mother upset and stuff." replied Curtis noticing his mother's reaction to Mr. Johnson's tone.

"Alright, alright you don't have to get all fussy. Here's a little something for your trouble. If you help me find my wife it will be more.

Ms. Byrd looked down in Mr. Johnson's hand and noticed it was a hundred dollar bill.

"Boy," Ms. Byrd pause slowly lifting her head up and seeing Mr. Johnson's pitiful face. "Keep your money, if she contacts me I promise to let you know."

"You promise."

"Yes, I said I promise. Hey at least you got money to take care of her."

"Well now its an agreement," Mr. Johnson said trying to force the hundred dollar bill in her hand.

Mr. Johnson walks out the door and Ms. Byrd, her son Curtis and Trish all looked at each other and motions their head in disbelief.

"He woulda had to ask me twice." Trish added for a laugh but deep inside she was serious.

They all started laughing out loud and Mr. Johnson suddenly walks back in the store.

They immediately stop the flow of the laugh and looks busy as Trish pulls her register and Curt opens the other register. Mrs. Byrd stares right at him.

"My fault, I forgot to leave you with this." Mr. Johnson extends his arm to give Mrs. Byrd a card with his number on it.

Mrs. Byrd takes it and Mr. Johnson walks back out the door.

Mr. Johnson is that You?

As Mr. Johnson was leaving the store walking to his car, he noticed another car pulling up beside him. In it was a young man who was staring at him. Mr. Johnson looked in the opposite direction to avoid eye contact.

"Mr. Johnson is that you?"

"Do I know you?" Mr. Johnson asked while stretching his neck forward to get a better look. "Oh, you are that man." He said remembering their encounter.

"I thought you dashed out of state somewhere." The staring man stated.

"Oh, I did but I came back."

"For what? Wait let me guess, a woman or some money, right?"

"Well you know I already got money." He bragged. "So it was a woman."

"Oh, I should have known."

"So tell me, what are you doing here?"

"I am here to see if my mother is ready." responded a curious Brent.

"Who is your mother, Mrs. Byrd!?" Mr. Johnson said sounding surprised.

"Yeah, how did you know that?" Brent asked with a return surprised expression.

"Man, man, man, it's really a small world. Your mother is my wife's church mother."

"Oh dang, I am glad I didn't do that to you then." Brent said making a fist and placing it around his mouth.

They both motioned their head without expression.

"You heard what happened to Ted the guy who tried to have you killed, right?"

"Yeah, what you mean I heard?" He responded in a sarcastic tone.

"Oh was that your doing?" he asked with one wide eye.

"Aye man I got to go. Take care alright."

Brent motions his head slowly. " He is lucky I don't owe Ted any promises." He said to himself.

Brent slowly walks to the grocery store door and sees his brother getting ready to lock it. His brother gives him a slanted smile when he sees him coming into the store.

They both give each other a nod when they establish eye contact.

"Hey, did you see that man?" asked Ms. Byrd when she sees Brent walking in the store.

"Yeah, I know that man."

"From where, he don't sale or do drugs do he?" she asked pulling out his card again to see his line of work.

"No Mama, I don't sale drugs or do them either."

"I know boy. I know you catching that money when it falls off those trees."

"Ha, ha, ha, you are so funny Mrs. Byrd. You are going to make me lose count." said Trish laughing while counting some twenties.

Here give me that card. I will keep it because I don't trust him." Curtis took the card and placed it under a drawer that he is getting ready to pull.

Trish glanced at where he placed the card and kept a mental thought as she continued to count.

"Anyway Momma, I went by the house and I realized you weren't at home and so I knew you was here. So I was wondering if you wanted me to take you home. This way you won't have to wait on Curtis." Hoping she will accept his invitation.

"Oh I don't mind waiting."

"Yeah, you can go. I got her." replied his brother with a gazed as he grabs the key from his waist to open another register.

"You got her, huh?" He responded with a smirk.

They both stare.

Trish grabs her register to go to a private area in the store. She felt the negative tension in the room and assumed an argument or a fight was about to start.

"Yeah, son don't start arguing with him. I will see you when I get home, alright."

Brent sighs and gives a slight glance at his brother again and turns around to exit out the door.

"You don't mind?" Brent blurted while grabbing a bag of chips off one of the counters.

Curtis was getting ready to go after him but Mrs. Byrd gives him a look. He noticed the look and agreed to let him go.

"Boy I can't wait until he go back to where he came from, Curtis said while reaching in his pocket to see if he got enough change to pay for the chips."

You didn't Kill the Cop.

Brent walks out the door smiling because he knows that he pissed his brother off when he took those chips. He gets a call while he is getting into his car.

"Who dis?" he answers.

"Hello, Brent?"

"Yeah, who is this?" he asked again not recognizing the voice.

"Hey, the detective is not dead."

"Oh, it's you…Well I know he didn't die." Brent was disappointed but he had a feeling he would be getting this call one day.

"So are you going to keep your promise or what?"

"I don't know. A brief pause, then he thought. "You know if someone tries to kill him now it's going to get back to you."

Another brief moment of silence as the doctor contemplates what he just said, "Well I guess you are right. Brent, how come you missed?"

"Dr. I thought I had a good shot although I was aiming 75 feet away at an angle with that hand gun I gave you."

"What! The one you gave me?" he repeated his comment hoping that he will get a 'no' answer.

"Yeah, that one."

"Dang, why didn't you say something?"

"For what? What's the big deal."

"Because, I think the cops got it now and if they trace the ballistics."

"What?" Brent screams dropping his jaw. "How did you let the cops get it? Boy you done did it now."

"Well never mind that." he starts thinking how Ted did him and wasn't interested in sharing that information. "I just hope my friend is able to keep his promise when the cops bring that to him. But anyway, since you couldn't help me out with that then how about telling me where I can get some drugs."

"Are you serious doctor?"

"Yes I am serious as a heart attack and trust me I am a doctor and I know how serious a heart attack can be."

"You don't have to be a doctor to know that." Brent replied sarcastically. "Anyway uh, you probably can get some at Rich Groceries after it closes."

"You talking about the one off of King's Street." He asked knowing of the area.

"Yeah, that one. I see you get around."

"Yeah, but Ted made a deal there and he double crossed me. I bet you he won't double cross me anybody more." The doctor said sarcastically. "But I am really going to miss his services."

"Yeah the drug dealing starts around 11:30 p.m. So if you get their around then, it shouldn't be a lot of traffic. Besides, I will call one of my boys to let him know that you will be coming so they won't think you are a cop."

"Aright Brent, now about the detective, I am not too worried about him. He still don't have nothing on me." The doctor said proudly.

"Alright, I still owe you one."

"I know and if he tries to go after me then." He inhales and exhales. "Then you must pay off your debt." He said lowing his tone.

I REMEMBER HIM NOW

Detective Mac lies in the hospital bed watching the T.V. The program Cops is about to come on.

"Bad boy, bad boy, what you gonna do. What you gonna do when it comes to you." Sang the T.V.

"Boy I wish they could have taped me when I was in uniform." He thought to himself as he watched a cop throw a suspect down to handcuff him.

Moments later his phone rings taking his attention from the television.

"Hello." he answered on the first ring.

"Hello, what are you doing today?" asked the person on the other end.

"Uh, watching cops." He replied wondering who was on the phone.

"Man how can you watch your job? I am sure all you're doing its critiquing them, right?"

"Yeah, you should have seen it yesterday when this cop tries to handcuff a man with one hand. Dah, go back to the academy, you know?"

"Oh, I guess that was stupid but you don't know why he was doing that. You know how things are when you are under the fire."

"Yeah, yeah, yeah. Anyway, what's up Officer? How can I help you, oh did you ever...."

"What, find out who that guy is?" Detective Billips asked completing his sentence for him..

"Yeah."

"Well it says in your notes that when you went to go see Dr. Cashion for the first time it was a curios person in the office with him. You later found out that that was Mr. Johnson."

"Oh, I remember him now, that day didn't he have."

"Have a son that the doctor helped?" Detective Billips completed his sentence again.

"Yeah, and stop finishing my sentences! "Anyway, I also talked to his wife on the phone."

"Oh, maybe I should have kept her here then."

"Well, it wasn't a long conversation. In fact, she hung up on me when I told her that Mr. Smith had a son."

"But, you think I can get something out of her, if I bring down the pressure."

"I don't know, but I guess she couldn't handle the pressure when she hung up the phone on me. Hold on." He says while a nurse comes in to check his vitals and asked for the arm he was holding the phone with. "I am back, what was I saying?"

"Well, you were saying something about some pressure but I know what I might do. Detective, when are you getting out of the hospital so I can give you this case?"

"Oh, I'll take it when I get out of here. Hold on again." Ma'am can you bring me some fresh cold water." He asked the nurse who was about to exit the room. "Yeah, I will take that case, no problem." He continued as he brought the phone back to his ear.

"Is that a promise?"

"Yeah it's a promise. Just keep me abreast on the case."

They hang up the phone and Detective Billips picks it back up to call Mrs. Johnson. He hears a tape recorder announcing that the phone is no longer in service. "Oh, that's odd." He thought. He then looks at the application Mr. Johnson had written on and signed. He noticed a cell phone number and no home number. Officer Billips dials the number. Somewhat surprised, the phone rings.

"Hello."

"Hello, Mr. Johnson, I need to talk to your wife."

"Hell, I do too. Have you seen her?"

"No, what do you mean?"

"Well, I mean that I came home and everything was gone." He replied throwing his free hand up in the air.

"Wow, that was quick. But I told her to stay in the area."

"I heard you when you said that. But do me a favor, if she gets in touch with you, will you call me?"

"Yeah right. I am no marriage counselor. You are on your own. Who knows why she is running from you anyway. What have you done?"

"Detective I don't know."

Detective Billips slowly motions his head in disbelief realizing no one ever knows what they did when their wife leaves.

"But I tell you what, if she contacts me, I will tell her you are very concerned."

"Yes I am, now what did you want with her anyway?"

"Oh." Detective Billips thought of something fast. "I wanted to share something the detective shared with me."

"What?"

"Sir, that's confidential. And speaking of the detective, he told me he ran into you one day coming out of a Dr. Cashion's office."

"Yeah, I remember that day. He looked at me kind of funny."

"What were you doing there?"

"I don't remember. Something to do with my son, I am sure."

"I can't wait until he gets this case back." Detective Billips said what he was thinking out loud.

"What you say? I hope you are not going to give the case back to him." Mr. Johnson replied in a panicking tone.

"Oops, he repleid realizing he said what he was thinking out loud. "Yeah I am, would you have a problem with that?"

Silence.

"IIcy, find out where your wife is and have her to give me a call." Detective Billips asked breaking the silence.

"Uh, she may contact you before she contacts me."

"You think?"

"Yes."

"Hopefully, that's the case. Good bye Mr. Johnson."

Please don't tell him

After checking into a room at Barry County Suites, Mrs. Johnson comes by Mrs. Byrd's home to have her to watch Fred while she takes care of some things. She just worried about Fred and didn't think it will be smart to leave him alone.

"Ding dong, ding dong, ding dong." She rings the doorbell. "Mrs. Byrd it's me, Sister Johnson." She informed her as she hears foot steps of someone walking towards the door.

"Hey, we were just talking about you to a girlfriend of mines on the phone." Mrs. Byrd said opening the door.

"Is that right, what y'all saying about me?"

"Nothing, we were just discussing how your man or ex came by the store trying to give me some money for your whereabouts."

"Wait a minute, how did my ex-husband know about you and that store." She asked with narrow eyes.

"Well, I think he just came in to get a snack and me and my son were talking about you."

"See you always gossiping." Mrs. Johnson said as irritated.

"Yeah, I know." She replied softly avoiding eye contact. "Anyway, what brings yall by?" she asked with a quick glance at Fred.

"Did you tell him anything?" asked Mrs. Johnson ignoring the question for now.

"No sister. Now tell me, why are you here?"

"Well ok." She said as she raised her brows and slowly turns her head away and back. "I was wondering if you can watch my boy so I can go and take care of Ted's funeral to pay him his last respect."

"Sure, he's not a bad kid, right."

"No, he's not and thank you. I am going to get him and his stuff out of the car."

Mrs. Johnson walks back in the house with his stuff and Fred walks in behind her with some head phones on listening to some hip hop rap. Fred has been listening to a lot of Rap music to take his mind away from his problems.

"You mind turning them off and taking them off your ear." Mrs. Johnson asked before she introduced Fred to Ms. Byrd.

"Here you go." She hands Fred a notebook and pencil. She promised to get Fred this to help him express his feelings. "Remember what we talked about on the way down when you told me that you sometimes feel very sad and angry about what you had done and I told you that you should express your feelings on paper? So here take it and just express yourself and how you feel about things on paper and I think this will help. It will be better than listening to that rap stuff."

"Can I write it like a rap song?" asked Fred looking up at Mrs. Johnson expressionless.

She lets out some wind before she speaks. "Dude I guess, as long as you get your feelings out, ok. Anyway, you treat Mrs. Byrd with the upmost respect, alright." She commanded Fred as he grabs the notebook and Mrs. Johnson not letting go until she established eye contact to get the assurance that he understands.

"Yes, ma'am."

"Show her the etiquette you learn at home."

Fred nods his head. *"Don't you think I am getting a little too old for this baby sitting stuff."* He thought as he nods, slightly smiling.

"Bye,…….. By the way, you know where the preacher is now?" Mrs. Johnson asked while straighting up Fred's things in a corner spot in the house.

"Well, I think he's at the church."

"Good, I am on my way down there now. I will see you at around six or eight."

"OK, take your time, I may go to the store and get some things."

"OK, make sure he wears his jacket, he already has a cold."

"Momma. Stop treating me like a little kid." Fred said out loud unable to keep this comment to himself this time.

"What! Boy you are not grown. Like I said, put your jacket on." replied Mrs. Johnson with a slight smirk on her face.

Fred looks at Mrs. Johnson walking out the door until she was out of sight. Then he turns to Ms. Byrd.

"Hey, that's going to be up to you. I am not going to make you do anything. I can only ask and hopefully you do what's right. You seem like a smart kid and you will do the right thing. In the mean time, I might have to take a little nap. Are you going to be ok?"

Fred nods.

"What, Sister Johnson didn't teach you manners."

"Yes ma'am."

"That's better. Anyway man you can sit out here on the porch and listen to your head phone set. I will be out soon to go to the grocery store. You got some money."

Fred nods again and Ms. Byrd gives him a sharp look.

"Yes ma'am." He quickly answered.

Meanwhile, Mrs. Johnson drives to the church and meets the pastor at the door.

"Praise the Lord, what wind blew you by?"

"The south wind, I am moving to Atlanta." Mrs. Johnson answered entertaining his sarcastic remark.

"O, what part?"

"Some where around Buck Head."

That's good, we got a dynamic sister church there.

"Yeah, I may join it once I get settled."

"But what brings you back here and did you get remarried?" asked the pastor raising his brow.

"Yeah, I did?"

"You know, I was kind of upset when I wasn't asked to do your wedding this time. I felt that you probably didn't want to trust me because of what happened at your first wedding. Did you ever hear about your first husband and his whereabouts? I mean did you just give up on him or what? Is he considered dead or alive since he has been missing? I will think you guys are still married, right?"

"Well, let's just say socially we may have been but legally we aren't. Anyway, I was wondering if you can do my husband's eulogy." She attempts to get down to business.

"What? What's going on? I am confused." asked the pastor scratching his head.

"It's a long story and I am sure if you call Ms. Byrd she will give you the gist of the story." She said folding her arms and looking at him with one wide eye.

"What and get more confused! Alright, and I understand if you don't want to talk about it right now. So what's up, have you made any arrangements for the funeral?"

"Well, it's going to be Friday at 11:00 o'clock in the morning at the Barry's Funeral Home."

"I will make sure I am there this time and when I get there I am going to stay put, if you know what I mean." He replied with a glare in his eyes.

"Please do that." she replied getting his hint as she gets up off the pew to exit the church the phone rings.

"Hey, I hope you don't mind letting yourself out and I will see you Friday, alright."

She nods.

God bless you sister. said the Pastor with a smile.

Why Didn't You Sign the Form

Mr. Johnson is just returning from a visit to the court house and after confirming that he wasn't married because the certificate wasn't signed by an ordained minister, he rushed to call 411 to find his number.

When the operator gave him the number he wasted no time calling the church.

"Hello, can I speak to the head pastor please? I forgot his name." he asked the person who picked up the phone.

"This is he. How can I help you?"

"Pastor, you didn't sign on my marriage certificate!"

"What?"

"I decided to take a trip down to the court house to see why my wife felt that she can get a divorce and get married without my permission. And they showed me the certificate without your signature."

"Wait a minute. Who is this? What marriage are you talking about?" the pastor asked confused but firm.

"I am Reggie Johnson, you married me and Felicia a while ago when you had that accident."

"Oh!" The pastor sound surprised. "She just left here, are you her ex-husband? When did you get back? Man you all got some talk show stuff going on here."

"What, she still in town? Where did she go? Where is she?" Mr. Johnson asked anxiously.

The pastor felt the anger in his voice and decided that he should back up with giving him information about Mrs. Johnson.

"Sir, I don't know. She didn't say. I have to go and get ready for a wedding. Oh, that reminds me, I am sure you know what I was going through at the time of that wedding, so I had my reasons why I couldn't sign it."

"Yeah, yeah, I know. But when my wife comes back, will you call me? I am sure the church needs a new roof, right?" he asked with a mischievous gleam in his eyes.

"Ahhh sir, we need more than that. But what are you saying?" the pastor replies folding his arms.

"I am just saying if you give me any information of her whereabouts, I will give you a lot of money to fix up the church."

"Thank you, but I think the sister's safety is worth more than my church. Besides, my sole wont be able to take it if something happens to her because of my doing."

"Pastor. Alright, what's your soul going to say when you let the roof fall down on your members?"

"Sir!" he responded biting his lips.

"Alright, alright here take my number in case you change your mind."

"Mister, I don't want your number, I meant what I said, what kind of preacher do you think I am? Good-Bye." said the pastor as he hangs up the phone and lets out some wind then walks to the back office to check the caller id and copies Mr. Johnson's number down. Just in case. He said to himself with a gleam and a quick glance to the ceilling.

So, What's Your Name

"You know, you remind me of my Step Father, Ted." Fred said to Brent during a conversation they were having on the porch as Ms. Byrd nods off.

Ms. Byrd felt asleep moments after Mrs. Johnson drops him off. Brent arrived moments later introduces himself and started a conversation with the boy. He was shocked when he heard that Fred was associated with Ted.

"Ted Humphrey?" Brent replied with wide eyes.

Fred nods.

"What? No wonder you are so cool." Silence as Brent takes in the news that he is Ted's son. "Stick around. I am going to show you some things." Brent added slightly smiling.

"Fred, are you still out there?" asked Ms. Byrd hearing Brent's voice.

"Yes, I am Ms. Byrd." Fred replied.

"Who are you out there talking to and what time is it?"

"Surprise, and its 6:35p.m." Brent said walking in the house and looking at his watch.

Ah shucks, I may have missed my bus to go to the store to get some cake mix for Curtis Birthday.

"I will take you mom. I guess." Brent said knowing he will get a no answer.

She stares off thinking about whether are not she should let him or not. "Well, I guess this time won't hurt. Let me get my things."

"Cool, we will be out here." Brent responded cheerfully.

"Alright, hey what the two of you been talking about anyway? Don't feed him all that crooked mess you are talking about."

"Momma, he's a cool boy and I am sure anything I share with him won't change him."

"Just don't corrupt his mind alright." She replied searching for her purse.

Brent's cell phone rings.

"So, have you ever killed someone?" he asked while taking a look at the phone number to see if he recognizes the number.

He takes another look at Fred and notices his eyes are watering up. "Boy what's wrong with you?" He asked while Fred quickly starts writing in his notebook to express his feelings as Mrs. Johnson told him to do. Brent never answers the call and puts the phone back on the belt hook. "You know you got to wipe those tears off. What are you writing anyway? Let me see."

Brent jokingly takes the notebook out of Fred's hands. Fred reaches back for it and Brent sweeps his hand away with his free arm. He quickly reads the paper on the notebook.

"Dag, this is tight! You got skills!" Brent said stunned by what he is reading. "How long have you been writing, man?"

"I just started today. Give it back, its private." Fred said reaching for the notebook. Yeah Mrs. Thomas told me to right my problems down but I decided to put them in a rhythm.

"Straight! Fred keep writing and expressing your feelings like this. You have a natural born talent and I am almost sure you will get picked up by somebody. A moment of silence as Brent looks at Fred for his acknowledgment. "Ima see if I can get you a contract. I know some people." Brent added as Ms. Byrd is coming out of the house.

"Are you all ready, where is, oh there you are." She suddenly sees Fred who turns around with a forced smile. "Are you ready, you didn't let my boy tell you anything bad did you?"

"No momma, come on now." Brent responded before Fred speaks. "Give me some kind of credit."

"Well, I am trying. That's why I am taking a risk now and letting you take me to the store. If no one comes to you asking for anything during the ride there, then you can take me other places as well."

Brent knew that he has been out the game for a while. So he knew this was an easy task.

They drove pass downtown to the store.

"I think my daddy used to work over there." Fred said while pointing at a building with the smoke coming out of it."

"Nah, a man we are not going to talk about Ted right now, alright." responded Brent remembering Ted's block.

I am not talking about Ted. I am talking about my real dad.

Mrs. Byrd gives him a nudge on his shoulder. "Boy, he's talking about his real dad." She repeated what he said and gave him an evil stare.

"Oh." Silence as Brent rides and sees plenty of old customers. He motions his head in disbelief of some of the people still in the streets.

"Hey Brent," someone screamed when they noticed him stopping at a stop light. Brent motions his head hoping the person keeps walking away. He can imagine what his mother is thinking.

"Just keep looking forward Brent, don't even acknowledge him." said Ms. Byrd noticing a man walking towards the car and smiling.

"Brent it's me Russ, what's up with you?"

Brent noticed the voice and turns around. It was one of his old friends who he brought up in the drug game.

"What's up Rusty, Can you see I am busy now."

"Ahhing that's so cool, you are taking your mother around. Who is that little boy, one of your new recruits?" he asked with a smile and quick glance at Fred.

Fred stares at the man without blinking.

"You listen to him, he showed me a lot when I was a teenanger."

"Man, I will see you, my light is changing."

"Alright, but you heard what happened to Ted, right?"

Brent nods his head as he zips through traffic.

Fred stares at the guy as something moves inside of him.

"Sorry, about that." Brent said as he glanced at his mother.

"Well son you handled that well. I am going to tell your brother that you are really trying to change."

Brent felt proud. Then he thought, *"why in the hell does she got to get his approval."*

"They pulled up in front of the store and Brent reaches over and gives his mom a hug with one arm. "Thanks mom for letting me take you." he said with a smile. I told you I was out of that stuff.

"Good son and stay out! Come on Fred lets go. You are not coming in to say hi to your brother."she asked Brent as she and Fred climbes out of the car.

"No, mom I have to get going. I will talk to him later."

Mrs. Byrd and Fred exit the car and walk towards the glass doors and see Trish with a broom sweeping out her area.

"Hey, Ms. Byrd, who you got there?" Trish asked as she stops the motion from sweeping.

"Hello, this is Fred, you mind watching him while I do a little shopping."

"No, I don't mind," Trish said while getting the seat the lazy cashier sits in. "Here you can sit here."

Fred sits down and Mrs. Byrd goes down the isle looking for the cake mix.

"So where are you from kid?"

"Well, I used to stay in the suburb on Barry Street. Now we are moving to Atlanta."

"Oh for real, what part?"

In the city somewhere.

Alright, I have a friend down there."

"What brings you here?"

"My mother is getting a funeral ready."

"Whose funeral," she asked picking up a bag of chips a customer left by her register.

"Ted, my dad or my step-daddy." Fred gets up and walks to her and hands her a fifty dollar bill.

"Wow, thank you for this, you just like that other guy who came in here flashing his money around."

"Who you all talking about Mr. Johnson." Mrs. Byrd asked when she overhears their conversation.

"Yes, I think that's his name."

"Yeah, that's his step daddy too."

"Dang, how many dads you got?" she asked looking at Fred with the fifty dollars still in his hand.

Fred offers her a little smile.

"What you want me to do with this fifty?" she asked holding it up towards the light on the ceiling checking to make sure it's not counterfeit. She then picks up a marker that lies next to her register.

"Give me change." He asked.

"Alright, is two tens, a twenty and a five, alright." She responded slashing the dollar with the marker.

Fred nods his head as he gradually narrow his eyes. "Wait a minute, you owe me another five, right." He said with a drop jaw and a smile.

"Just seeing if you are up on your game. Here." She hands him another five with a smile.

"Ms. Byrd, wasn't that guy looking for them?" Trish asked as she closed her drawer.

"Well he was mainly looking for his wife but wherever Fred is, he may find his wife.

"Oh, but Fred is with you now?" she curiously asked as she picks the broom back up.

"Yeah, until his mom comes back to get him."

"Oh." She responded looking at the cash register where Curtis put that card with Mr. Johnson's number on it.

Where Can We Meet

When Trish made it home from work, the first thing she grabs is her home phone to call Mr. Johnson.

"Hello, you don't know me but I think I know where your wife is."

"What do you mean? Who is this?"

"This is Trish from the store. Are you still talking about paying a person that gives you information? Where your wife is?"

"Yeah, whatever, where is she?"

"Wait a minute, hold your horses. Can we meet?"

"Where, where can we meet?" stuttered Mr. Johnson throwing his free hand up in the air as he was getting anxious and frustrated at the same time.

"You can just meet me back at the job."

"At the store? Suppose somebody sees you?"

"Huh, you let me worry about that. Now how about you meet me in the next two hours or so? I need some time to take a shower because I am going out after you give me the money. How much are you planning on paying me anyway?"

"I don't know, how much you want?"

She starts thinking of the price of a purse she saw at the mall. She quotes it.

"$350.00 dollars"

"Alright hurry up, don't have me waiting."

"I won't, good-bye."

After they hung up the phone, Mr. Johnson looks in his wallet to see if he has that amount in his pocket. He did. And meanwhile, Trish finished taking her shower and crawls out and puts on a nice fitted dress. They both climbed into their cars and drove towards the grocery store.

Now, Mr. Johnson is in his car waiting and thinking about the time he met Brent here. Minutes later a car pulled up taking his thought away.

"Oh, I am sorry, I thought you was somebody else that I was suppose to be meeting." said the man in the car.

Mr. Johnson motions his head with a smile and the man drove across the parking lot. That man's mistake confirms to Mr. Johnson that Rich's groceries parking lot must be the hot meeting place for people in this neighborhood. Another car pulled up next to Mr. Johnson. "You cool?" the man expressed holding up a piece sign.

Mr. Johnson nods his head assuming that the man wanted him to buy some drugs. He stares at his shiny rims as he drove off. He then takes a look at his watch.

"What is take…." Before he finishes the question, he sees someone in a small two door car that looks like the girl he saw at the store.

She slows down narrowing her eyes to make sure its Mr. Johnson. Mr. Johnson gives her the Okay signal. She stops the car in front of Mr. Johnson and gets out the car before Mr. Johnson gets completely out. He noticed the fitted dress.

"Wow. Girl, I didn't know you were that hot." He said with a smile.

"Yeah, I have clothes on at the grocery store because it gets cold ass hell sometimes."

"Oh, but anyway where is my wife?"

"Mister where is my money? You know like that movie, show me the money." She blurted with an eager grin.

Mr. Johnson reached for his wallet and pulled out the exact amount.

"Here!" He said seriously.

Thank you. She replies while spreading the three hundreds and the fifty with her thumb and index finger to get a quick count. She then folds the money up and opens her designer purse and places the money in her wallet. "Now, do you know where Mrs. Byrd stays?"

"No, I never have been over her house."

"Well I tell you what you can do, follow me and don't tell her I showed you where she stays because I need my job."

Mr. Johnson nods his head.

Trish turns around after she gives Mr. Johnson a brief stare to show that she meant what she said.

Mr. Johnson gives her one back and when she turns around he looks down and noticed how the dress fits her body.

"Girl, if I wasn't married." He mumbled. "*Am I still married,*" he wondered to himself realizing that the pastor needs to sign the papers.

Trish suddenly drives by as Mr. Johnson makes a U-turn to follow her.

Moments later, Trish slows down when she got to one of the neighborhood streets. Mr. Johnson sees Trish pointing at one of the houses on the block. When Mr. Johnson looked as if he was turning in one of the driveways, Trish gave him the ok and drove off. When Mr. Johnson got to the door and rang the doorbell, he rang it like a mad man.

"Ding dong, bang, bang, bang, ding dong, ding dong, bang!"

"Who in the……….boy who ever you are, you are trying to make me lose my religion. Banging on my door like you got a problem. Who is it?" Yelled Mrs. Byrd coming from the hall.

"Ms.Byrd, it's me, is my wife in there?"

"Boy, how did you know your wife was over here? She responded while unlocking the door and opening it while not unlocking the screen.

"Is my wife here?" Mr. Johnson asked again this time looking firmly in Mrs. Byrd's eyes.

"Young man, your wife came and left two hours ago."

"Where did she go?"

"I don't know, she didn't say."

There was a moment of silence while Ms. Byrd looks at Mr. Johnson and his pitiful looking expression.

"Young man, you need to just move on with your life, apparently she don't want you no more and plus she got remarried on you too. What more does she have to do?" she said holding the door as if she is getting ready to close it at anytime.

"Damn, are you sure she didn't say where she was going?" said Mr. Johnson without commenting on her comment.

Ms. Byrd motions her head to say no. "That's sad. I just told you she was remarried." she said while closing the door when Mr. Johnson momentarily looks away.

Mr. Johnson walks away and drives around to look for her for a brief time and later goes home for the night.

"The first thing I am going to do tomorrow is go down to the court house to get a copy of my certificate." Mr. Johnson told himself before falling asleep.

The Dumb Look

Mr. Johnson goes to the city hall to get a copy of his marriage certificate. He noticed where it wasn't signed by a ordained minister. "So if I take this down to the minister and get him to back date it, then I will be married officially." He asked the clerk at the desk.

She nods.

He takes the certificate back to the minister.

He arrives at the church.

"Hello Minister," he yelled when he sees the minister about to leave.

"Sir for you not to be a regular member here, you sure knows how to catch me." replied the minister while locking the door. "Well anyway, are you still looking for your wife or what?"

"Yes, but first I would like to make sure she is my wife. Here, can you sign this?"

"What you got there?" he narrows his eyes looking at the form Mr. Johnson is presenting to him. "Is that a marriage certificate?"

"Yes, it's me and my wife's marriage certificate. Can you sign right here and backdate it for May 22, 1993."

"Is that deal for the new roof still available?" he asked with a mischievous smile.

"Sir, that was a deal for telling me the whereabouts of my wife."

He takes the form from his hand. "I am sure we can work something out. Go ahead write the check out with my name. I don't want to put this against the church."

Mr. Johnson pulls out his checkbook from his back pocket. "How do you spell your name?" the pastor gives him a brochure he had in his briefcase. Hey, go ahead and tell me where she is while I am writing this check out."

"You know there are a lot of cops at funeral homes." The pastor said in a attempt to keep his salvation as he hopes he gets the point.

"OK, your point?" Mr. Johnson asked lending his neck forward while still writing the check. He completes the check and before Mr. Johnson lets the check go. "Tell me where she is," he asked with no expression.

Because of the promise he made with Mrs. Johnson to not tell the pastor didn't want to go back on his word. But he knew how bad the church needs the roof and a lot of other things. He thought of another way to tell him without exactly going back on his promise. God forgive me for my sins. "Brother, let this go, I got to go and get prepared for a funeral tomorrow at 11:00 a.m. at the funeral home on Baker."

The pastor gives him a dumb looking expression.

Mr. Johnson noticed his look and got the clue by giving him a slight smile.

Don't I Know You

While Mr. Johnson is parked on a side street, he notices someone walking by with a sling on his arm staring at him. The stranger walks over to get his attention.

Knock, knock, knock, he knocks on the windshield.

Mr. Johnson noticed who the guy was and scoots down trying to become inconspicuous.

"Don't I know you?" asked the man in the sling arm.

"I don't think so," Mr. Johnson responded.

"You mind if I ask you your name."

Mr. Johnson thought of the first name that came to his mind.

"I am Mike Jones." He didn't realize that he just subsconciencly heard that rapper's song on the radio when some teens pull up next to him at a light.

"O'kay, responded the detective in disbelief. "Well I am Detective MacIntosh and sorry to disturb you."

The detective walks away. But before he leaves, he takes a look at the license plates to run them in.

He calls the dispatcher on his cell phone.

"Hello dispatcher, this is the detective can I get you to run these plates?" he whispers into his phone.

"Sure, what is it?"

"X-ray, Apha, Boy 126."

"Are they from here?"

"Oh, that's affirmative."

"Alright, give me a minute."

While he waits, he stands by some officers directing traffic. He notices the limousine coming in front of the convoy. When the limousine parked, the chauffer opened the door to let a lady and a little boy out.

"Can you believe that he had just got married to her?" One of the officers directing traffic said to Detective Mac who was standing right beside him.

"Are you serious? Is that her boy?" asked Detective Mac.

"Yeah, I think so."

"Wow, Ted didn't tell me that he was going to get married but he did tell me he was thinking about adopting a boy."

"Well, I know if I had a woman like that it wouldn't be no secret if I was getting married." He smirks.

"Poor Ted, it seems as if he was trying to get his life back in order." the detective said as he stares off at the pallbearer lifting the casket.

"But you know what's weird? When they gave us the address to go pick her up, it was the same address of the house he supposedly broke into. So, how can that guy get shot for breaking in his own house?"

"Oh, that's where I know that guy from." Detective Mac said as he suddenly pays more attention to the cop.

His phone rings.

"Hello, detective that plate ran as a Reginald Johnson on 2116 Barry Street." announced the dispatcher.

"Thank you, I remember him now." He said loud enough for the officer directing traffic to hear it.

"Oh sir, we went to pick her up at a Mrs. Byrd house after we waited for them at the house she was staying at. I think I was told that she was not interested in getting picked up at the house her husband was murdered."

"Sir, can you call in the officers to keep an eye on that car park over there in that block. We might have a stalker on our hands." He commanded rotating his eyes back and forth at the car Mr. Johnson was sitting in and then back at the officer.

"Yes sir." he replied while snatching his radio from his belt.

Meanwhile, the detective walks in behind the family. He looks around and sees a lot of familiar faces of people that he arrested before and some ex-cons and some drug dealers, including the ones that ran away when he caught Ted and made that agreement.

After the pastor finished preaching and had everybody to walk around this one person that was holding up the line stops and lets out a loud cry. The people in the congregation looked at each other and shrugged their shoulders to display that they didn't know who that person was. However, some ushers helped the lady up and back to her seat.

"Man, I didn't know." Russ stopped the line flow, turns and looks at Brent and Fred who were sitting on the front pew. Brent was staring off at the crying woman who was being escorted. The lady looked very familiar to him though.

He then turns around with a surprised look on his face to the guy standing behind him, "why, why didn't you tell me?"

"Russ, I didn't get a chance to tell you with so much going on."

One of the ushers kindly asked them to keep the line going by extending their hand.

Later, back at the funeral reception, Fred runs into Brent and Russ again.

"Aye Fred man I didn't know that Ted was your father. I would have given you my condolences when I met you when you were riding with Brent and his mother the other day. Blame it on Brent, he should have told me."

"Hell, I just found out that day myself." Brent responded sprinkling salt on his meal.

"Anyway, Fred, me and Ted go back a long way. In fact, when I was about your age, he was one of my role models. Yeah, I never told him this. I was amazed how he never went to jail for some of the things he used to get away with. It was almost like he had the police on his side. Anyway, if you ever want to do what I do, I will be ready to teach you the game."

Fred glances at him with a smirk as he puts some macaroni in his mouth. Suddenly, Mrs. Johnson walks to the table.

"Fred you are welcome to sit with the family. Unless you just want to sit with your friends." She asked glancing at Brent and Russ.

"I know you, but who are you?" pointing at Russ.

"I am a good friend of Ted."

"OK, but who are you?" she replied shrugging her shoulders.

"I am Russ."

"Oh, I am Mrs. Humphrey. Fred again the offer still stands if you want but if you want to stay here, I will be okay with that."

Fred looked back at the head table and noticed all elders at the table.

"I am cool." He said after taking a swallow of the macaroni he just put in his mouth.

Mrs. Johnson nods as she walks back to her seat.

"Mrs. Johnson, before you go back, do you know who that lady was that was crying like she just lost her child. O yeah you know what? I think that was his mother. Is she here?"

"I wanted to find out who she was for sure. She did look a little like the pictures I saw of her. Where did she go?" she asked looking around the room. "You know Ted told me that after she realized that Ted can take care of himself, she found another man and never looked back. Ted said that she wanted to leave and start over again. In fact, that was our plan. She said as she turns away from the table to avoid the embarrassment of water filling up in her eyes.

When Mrs. Johnson got out of ear shot, Russ decided to pick up the conversation where they left off.

"So are you really going to pick up where your daddy left?"

"Yeap. I kind of owed it to my boy Ted for what I did before I left. So I will teach you." Brent said before Fred can answer.

"Oh alright. What did you do?" Russ said.

"Ah dude, that's between me and Ted." Brent said firmly.

"You promise huh? Alright, we are in church." Brent said with a slight smile.

"I would have betted you, but we are in a church."

"Alright, I feel you." Brent replied as he took a bite of his chicken.

"Fred, what's wrong. Why you not eating?"

"My stomach hurts." He said holding his stomach.

"Oh, you just upset about Ted, huh?" Brent wondered.

"No, I am alright. I think he's with my daddy now."

The table was silent as they respect his statement.

Meanwhile, Mrs. Johnson finished her meal and got up meeting the rest of Ted's family. The detective approached Mrs. Johnson. "Hello, Mrs. Johnson you don't know me but we talked on the phone awhile ago."

Mrs. Johnson looks at him with a blank stare as if to say *"And?"*

84

"Well anyway, my name is Detective Macintosh."

Her posture changed as the name went through her spine.

"First of all, sorry for the loss of your husband Mr. Johnson, I mean Mr. Hughes. Well I think I just ran into your other husband out there.

Mrs. Johnson lifted her eyelids as far as they will go.

"Don't worry I got my boys looking out for him. Anyway here is my card. Call me if you want to help me clear some things up. I will be contact with you later."

"Dude, Can you see I am grieving. What's your badge number? Coming here and disrespecting his funeral. How dare you to come here talking that mess! Just make sure your boys watch out for Mr. Johnson, there is no telling what he will do to get to me. He is like a sociopath." said Mrs. Johnson in an angry tone.

"I mean are you fearing for your life."

"No. I don't think that's my concern but the man feels that he is above the world and nothing can touch him when it's time to get what he wants."

"Has he been stalking you?"

"No, he is not supposed to know I am here."

"Well apparently he knows. We caught him right outside in the car at your other husband's funeral." He said sarcastically.

"Sir, I only got one husband." she responded rolling her eyes at him.

"OK, the cops will stay here in case something goes down."

Mrs. Johnson nodded her head. "Can I get back to focus on his family now."

"Alright."

Later Mrs. Johnson and Fred were exiting the building and saw the police were holding someone.

"Felicia, tell them that I am your husband." Asked Mr. Johnson being held by two officers.

The crowd roared in disbelief.

Look I got our marriage license right here. He reaches to pull out the folded paper in his back pocket with his free hand.

"Whoa, whoa, whoa." The cops shouted getting ready to draw their weapon when they saw him reaching in his pocket.

Boldly ignoring the cops reaction, he pulls out the folded paper with the pastor's new signature on it.

Look at the signature part, do you see the part where the pastor was supposed to sign." asked Mrs. Johnson. See what happens when you try to fix things? He never signed it so we were never married.

"But it's signed."

"What?"

"Officer get that for her to see it." Detective Mac asked one of the free officers.

She takes it in her hand and looks and sees where the pastor signed and back dated it.

"You see, this is bull. How much did you pay someone for this signature? Is the pastor here?"

Mr. Johnson gives her a stare as if he was in a daze. "Come on, lets be a family again." He added with conviction.

Mrs. Johnson looks at Fred who is standing with Brent and Russ. Fred shrugs his shoulders.

"Officer, let him go, we got some talking to do."

The officers slowly let him go.

"You mind if I take you all home?"

"Dude it's not that easy. We need some time to talk to find out who you are now. I don't know if you are my same husband or not." Mrs. Johnson said looking directly in his eyes.

"You mind taking Fred with you." Mr. Johnson asked Brent as he hands him a fifty.

"Man." Brent said looking at the fifty as if he has just been insulted.

"Oh, alright. Mr. Johnson said noticing his reaction and reached back into his pocket and pulls out a one hundred dollar bill.

"That's better." Brent smiled as he turned around to escort Fred to his car.

"Mr. Johnson knew what kind of business Brent was into from his past involvement with him. But he didn't care at the time. He just wanted to be with his wife. Besides there is a little animosity towards Fred because he thinks that bullet that killed Ted was meant for him."

"Will you take him back over Mrs. Byrd's house for me?" Mrs. Johnson asked thinking that Fred was cool with it because he smiled when Mr. Johnson asked Brent to take him.

Brent nods his head in agreement.

Fred You are not Going to Believe This

Brent, Fred and Russ who was in the back seat drove around the neighborhood with no clue desination in mind. They are having a conversation.

"Aye man what do you think about them hooking back up on the day Ted is getting buried? That's kind of disrespectful don't you think?"

"If you knew what happened and why they were separated, then you would understand."

"Are you saying that Ted got something to do with them being separated from the start."

"Yeah, something liked that."

"You see, that's why I liked Ted, he always goes for what he wants."

"Yeah, but this time he may have paid for it deeply. But anyway, what about those good times we had with him." Brent continued trying to lift the conversation up for Fred.

"Like when he helped me to understand about being a man of my word. He said a man word is all he got and if he loses that, then he lost a lot. So Fred like he shared with me, be a man of your word." Russed said hitting Fred on the shoulders to get him to turn around to make sure he heard him and understands

Silence filled the car and moments later Russ sees someone who owes him money.

"Aye man pull over and let me out right here." He said scooting over to the door he was getting ready to get out of. As he was scooting, he noticed a notebook on the seat in his way. He picks it up. "Is this Fred's writing?" he asked thumbing through the pages.

"Oh yeah that's it, check that out." Brent said glancing in the rear view mirror in the back seat to see Russ with the notebook in his hand.

"Alright, hold on to it, I will check it out later. I will get home." Russ asked with his hand on the door level getting ready to dash out to catch that person.

Brent pulls over and Russ quickly opens the door and runs out. "I will holla." He yelled closing the door and jogging to catch the person he saw."

"So you like being called Little Ted." Brent asked Fred.

"No."

"Why not?"

"I am not worthy. I shot him." Fred said forcing back in the car seat.

"Ah man?" a sudden thought arrives in Brent's head. That day when that happened were you in the house Ted was in."

Fred sat in the seat dumbfounded wondering if he should entertain this stupid question.

"Were you?" Brent said again not liking the silent treatment.

"Man I was there, how you think I shot him." Fred said getting frustrated. "Can we talk about something else."

"Not yet stay with me brother. Now what gun did you use?"

"I used the family gun. But the gun they showed me wasn't the one I shot him with."

"Ah man that's deep." The car grew silent as Brent relates to what probably had happened. "Fred you are not going to believe this." Brent suddenly changes his mind because now the gun that shot Ted came from him. "Who is your real father?" he asked curious of the doctor and Fred's relation.

"His name was John Smith." Fred said expressionless.

"Is your father John Smith!?" Brent repeatedly asked in a shocking tone.

Fred looks at Brent and nods.

"Ah dang?" he said making a fist around his mouth with his free hand.

"Did you know him?" Fred asked never taking his eyes away from him.

"No, not really. Dang this is a small world."

"What, what you know?"

"Fred, how do you like staying with the Johnsons."

"It's cool but it's something about Mr. Johnson that I don't like. I mean I use to like him but as I grew older and learn some things, there is something about him that I don't like.

"Oh, I think I know what that something is."

"Brent, what's going on? Why are you talking as if we are playing fill in the blank?

"Tell me, did your daddy die in St. Martin's Hospital?" he asked with a quick glance at him as he smash on the brakes swiftly making a stop because a car just pulled in front of him.

Fred nods. "So did my mother!" he said after Brent gains his composure back.

"Yeah, I know. When I was locked up this doctor told me all about how he took a donor part and got paid for it. I think......He stop the flow as he takes a look at Fred and thinks of his feelings. "Hell. Do you know a Dr. Cashion?" he asked to add some more meat to his perception.

"Fred nods again."

"Oh my, oh my, Fred you are not going to believe this. This is messed up. But before I do, tell me, Mr. Johnson had a son didn't he?

Fred nods his head.

"He was about your age, right?"

He nods his head again.

"Well looks as if you aren't the only one killing people."

Fred looks at him with narrow eyes.

"A Fred I think........"

Suddenly, Brent hears the brief siren noise coming from a squad car.

"All man, you got your seat belt on." He asked as he looked at Fred who was putting it on at the same time he asked. He put his on too as he looked in the review mirror.

Momentarily, the cop exits his vehicle and approaches the vehicle. "License and proof of insurance. Asked the uniform cop with his hat pulled over his head almost covering his eyes. "I am pulling you over because you don't have a seatbelt on and it's against the law in this state."

Brent reached into his glove department and the police stared intensively at every movement of his hands. He hands the information to the cop who is wearing a slight smile because being stereotypical, he can't believe that he has the information he asked for.

As he was walking back to his squad to check his ID, he suddenly gets an emergency call in from the station. He returns back to Brent's car.

"Here's your information back. I just got an emergency over the radio. So it's your lucky day." He said rushing the information back in Brent's hand.

"What were you getting ready to say?"

"Uh, just put it like this, you didn't kill your daddy Ted."

"What!" Fred said with a curious expression. "How you know?"

"Man, was anybody else at the house that day?"

"Other than Mr. Johnson and Mrs. Johnson, no." Then he thought about that day harder. Oh, you know what._____ I did run into somebody when I ran out the door.

"Well you know who it was?"

"No, I was too scared."

"Well that's who shot Ted."

"What! So I didn't shoot him after all huh. Why nobody told me that?"

"Man, it's a lot going on that is too much for you right now and it may be better if I give you bits and pieces of the story, alright."

Silence filled the car again and Brent takes a glance at Fred's disappointed looking face.

"Aye Fred, check this out. If they got back together then you should act as if you don't know a thing, alright."

Fred sits still as he crosses his arms and stares off in a daze.

"I am sure you don't want to go back to a foster home right. Hell, I heard about those homes."

Fred starts thinking about the foster home he was in and he starts thinking of that day he first met them in the cafeteria.

"Does Mrs. Johnson know about this?" Fred asked turning away from the deep daze and focusing on Brent's answer.

"I doubt it. I mean she is a church going girl. So I know she won't be apart of this evilness."

Fred takes his eyes back off of him and goes back into his daze.

They arrived back at Mrs. Byrd's home.

"Son where did you find him?"

"At the funeral, Mr. Johnson showed up. You should have been there."

"I wish I was there now, but your brother was sick and I figured he needed me."

"What!" he replied in disgust. Anyway, the people came out and Mr. Johnson starts spilling the beans about how much he loved her and stuff."

"Well shucks, maybe I should have been there, that sounds like some juicy gossip." Mrs. Byrd said smiling.

"Yeah, it was. Sorry you missed it. So anyway, I have to watch Fred until they patch things up. Can he stay over here?"

"But your brother's sick, I don't want him to get sick too. She should have called me." She said with a questionable tone.

"I'll just take him with me for now."

"Alright, you've changed right?" Mrs. Bryd asked with a conspicuous look on her face as she was hoping that he don't get Fred in any trouble.

"Yeah, don't worry."

Fred hops back in the car with Brent and they drive away.

This is Between You and God

"Hello, Ms. Byrd can you keep Fred over night? I will bring him a change of clothes first thing tomorrow morning."

"Oh, he is out with Brent now, but my son is sick."

"Oh yeah, how sick is he?"

"Well his fever's coming down and it may be all the way down by the time Brent brings him back. But next time Sister Johnson asked me first before you just assume and make other plans."

"Alright, sorry things are happening so quickly." She replied throwing her hands up.

"Yes, I heard what happen at the funeral, where is he?"

"In the bedroom."

"What? On the same day your husband is getting buried?"

"Mother Byrd, he's my husband too."

"Sister, this is between you and God, you and God." she repeated using her free hand to point up at the sky.

"Mother I got to go. Can you tell Fred that I will be there to pick him up at around ten tomorrow morning?"

"Okay sister, God bless you."

"Thank you and you too."

"Honey, you off the phone?" Mr. Johnson yelled from the bedroom.

"Yeah, do you need it?"

"Yeah, I need to call Dr. Cashion real fast to tell him Detective Mac is back on the case."

"Dejavo.," Mrs. Johnson thought.

He makes the call.

"Hello Doctor, guess who is back?"

"What. What are you talking about?."

"OK, Detective Mac is back and I think he's working the case again."

"You mean to tell me that this wasn't an open and closed case."

"I wish, apparently they got suspicious when Fred didn't recognize the gun he shot and the ballistics on the gun matched the gun that shot the detective.

"That Brent!" He lets out some wind.

"Who you say?_____ Brent the hit man?" Mr. Johnson asked marking his statement.

"Yeah, how do you know him?"

"I met him in the last story of this book. figure of speaking." He said sarcastically.

"Oh, well he was one of my buddies in jail. Anyway, now what about the Detective?"

"Oh yeah, about the Detective. He came to Ted's funeral."

"Well I am not surprised because it was upsetting how I found out that they were working together."

"I know, but I don't think he came because they were friends."

Silence forms on the phone as the doctor is still waiting to hear why he came. "OK so, why did he come?" he grew anxious.

"I think he came to the funeral to get more evidence on the case. That's when I ran into him."

"Uh, what were you doing there?"

"To get my wife back!"

"Oh, she disrespected you and went to that guy's funeral, too." The doctor asked in disbelief.

"Yeah, I know but we had to solve some unfinished business; everything is straight now."

"Okay, but I don't think I will want my wife after I found out she has been with another man.

"Doc, are you married?"

"No, I am divorced."

"Right, so why should I listen to you?"

"Whatever, where is the boy? A brief second went by. He snaps his fingers. "Fred?"

"Out with Brent's mother."

"What, you know Brent and his mother?" he responds with a drop jaw.

"Yeah, Brent's mother is the mother of my wife's church. But, I didn't know Brent then."

"I know, it's kind of funny how this all came together."

"I hope Brent don't put two and two together." The doctor said as he shared a lot of information about the crime with Brent.

"What you mean?" Mr. Johnson asked wondering why the concern.

"I told Brent what happened at the hospital because we were like jail buddies."

"What, I shared a lot about the situation to him too."

"Do you think he knew John Smith?"

"Well Ted knew him, so he may have known him too."

"Well hopefully he won't share our involvments with the murder of his dad to him."

"But speaking of Brent, can you have him to call me as soon as possible? We got some unfinished business to take care of." Dr. Cashion said thinking about the detective.

I Guess the Saga Continues

Detective Mac is back at the office collecting more evidence that he got from Detective Billips, who was on the case until Detective Mac was discharged from the hospital.

"So we have the gun that shot me and Ted but no suspect or person for either of the cases. said Detective Billips who is going over the case with him. Well, Fred was supposed to have shot Ted." But when we showed him the gun, he was supposed to have shot him with, Fred looked dumb founded."

"Were there any finger prints on the gun?"

"No, I think the finger prints were wiped off."

"OK. You know, what? I am not going to let this case linger on like the last one did, we will get to the bottom of this real soon." He picks up the phone and calls Mr. Johnson's cell phone.

"Hello." Mrs. Johnson hurried to answer Mr. Johnson phone thinking it may be the other person who was with him at the time he was away.

"Don't answer my phone." Mr. Johnson said from some distance, kind of worried that it may be the woman he had gotten pregnant.

"This might be Fred now hold on." She said as she covers the mouth piece with her free hand and puts it down away from her ear. "Hello." she answers putting the phone back to her ear.

"It sounds like I caught you all at a bad time."

"Yes you did, who is this?" asked Mrs. Johnson with a hint of emotions.

"This is Detective Mac and I am going to need to ask you all some questions."

"Hold on." asked Mrs. Johnson as she puts her hand back over the phone. "It's Detective Mac saying that he needs to ask us some questions."

"Tell him we are busy and we will talk to him tomorrow or sometime."

"Alright, Detective can we talk tomorrow?" Mrs. Johnson asked listening to the commands from her husband.

"Sure. Is eleven in the morning alright."

"Alright. I guess that's alright." Mrs. Johnson replied getting irritated because she has to go back through this again.

"Are you guys still at the same place?" he asked.

"Well. Hold on." She puts the cell phone down and cover the mouth piece again as she sees Mr. Johnson walking into the room where she is standing. "Do you want me to tell him where we are?" she whispered to Mr. Johnson.

"Go ahead, because I am not going back to that police station."

Mrs. Johnson nods.

"Well, we are at Barry County Suite's Room 251."

The detective grins again. "We said eleven o'clock right?" he asked holding his grin.

"Yeah dude eleven." Mrs. Johnson looked at Mr. Johnson to make sure he heard the time and agreed.

"Goodbye Mrs. Johnson." The detective salutated still able keep his professionalism.

Mrs. Johnson hangs up the phone and turns to look at Mr. Johnson with irritation in her eyes.

"Come on baby, don't let the detective take our moment now. Everything is going to be alright. I will fix this." Mr. Johnson said without an expression.

"Noooooooo!" Mrs. Johnson yells knowing that everytime he says that, it means trouble.

McDonald's and a Movie III

Meanwhile Brent and Fred are still riding around. Brent thought he will continue to show Fred where Ted used to deal.

"Now over here is where we all use to gather and talk about hoes, oops I mean girls and our money. But that all got busted up when the cops rolled up and took me to the station for questioning."

"You know, although he never told me, I know that Ted got busted that day with something."

Silence filled the car as Brent ponders that day. "My Dad used to work at that building."

"Oh yeah, you told me that. You are talking about John right?"

Fred nods. "He used to come home very filthy." He added with his nod.

"Hey, I am getting tired of driving. Are you hungry?"

"A little, I didn't eat that much at the funeral." Fred said holding his stomach. "For some reason I think Russ makes my stomach turn because after he left I did feel a little hungrier."

"How do you know it's not because of what just happened to Ted?" asked Brent a little worried about Lil Ted.

"Because people who I am close too have died on me before and total different feeling when I am around Russ."

"Well Russ might be a good thing in your life so until you understand your feelings, I say ignore them for now. You know what I am saying?"

Fred nods looking straight ahead and Brent glances and sees his head movement.

"So guy, how do McDonald's sound to you and afterwards we can go catch that new movie I want to see."

Fred quickly looks at Brent wondering why does McDonalds and a movie keep coming up somehow. Then Brent's cell phone rings.

"Hello." Brent answered.

"Hello, Brent. This is your mom. Where are you?"

"Me and Fred are about to go to McDonald's then a movie after that."

"Oh, ok. Well, his mother just called and looks like she is getting back with her ex-husband and she suggested that Fred spends the night and she will be over first thing tomorrow."

"Cool, will it be ok to take Fred to the movies, then?"

"Yeah, I guess as long as it's a decent movie and not a lot of violence and sex."

"Good, his phone beeps alerting him another call is coming in. Well momma, we will be home right after the movies alright."

"You know it's a shame that you couldn't hang with your younger brother Curtis like that."

"Momma, me and Curt are on two different pages now. Now I have to go and take this call alright.

"Bye son."

Brent clicks over and takes in the fact that she called him son and not on his case for something. His phone beeps again.

"Yo, who this?"

"Brent, this is Russ."

"Where you at Bro?"

"About to pull in McDonald's with Fred."

"Straight, well come and get me."

"I thought you were going to find another ride home."

"Come on man, help me out. Besides, I got some information to share with Little Ted. I think I can do something for him." He said lifting the notebook up he had in his hand.

"I told you. Man, if I come get you, please try not to bring up Ted. I mean that's all we been talking about."

"That's cool, just come and get me where you dropped me off."

"Alright, we just going to go through the drive through, alright." He turned with cell phone to his ear to look at Fred to let him know that he was talking to him.

Fred nods.

"Can you bring me a number 2 back?"

"Dang, you are a little needy motha!"

"Man, I got your money." Russ responded quickly.

"Yeah, because you can give that money to Fred for his movie ticket."

"Oh, we are going to the movies too?"

"Man, I didn't say anything about a "we." What you taking a French class or something? Brent said jokingly. "But yeah, me and Fred are going to see that new movie *The Agreement.*"

"Good! That's the exact movie I wanted to go see. Let me go, alright."

"Man whatever, just be standing where I dropped you off."

"Alright peace."

When Brent hunged up, he turns and look at Fred again. "See I told you that Russ might me a good thing for you, he think he can do something for yah."

Fred slightly glances at Brent and smirks.

We Got Nothing to Hide

It's the next day and the detective is knocking on the Johnson's hotel door.

"Honey get that, I am brushing my teeth." yelled Mrs. Johnson after she takes a spit.

"Alright, who is it?" Mr. Johnson yelled at the door.

"It's Detective Mac."

"Oh dang, that's right." Mr. Johnson said just remembering the appointment they made with him. "Hey, it's the detective." He yelled in the direction of Mrs. Johnson.

"Oops, that's right," she said after another spit from her mouth wash. She dries her hand and mouth and then she walks in the bedroom and closes the bedroom door to get dressed. "I guess you can let him in, we got nothing to hide." she said slipping a skirt on.

"Alright, detective excuse the place. We had kind of a party last night." Mr. Johnson said with a proud look letting him in.

"Yeah, I was at the funeral." he responded with a slight grin back and looking at Mr. Johnson picking up a pillow from off the floor.

"Here, have a seat." Mr. Johnson said as he picked up some garments he had lying on a chair in the room.

"Thank you sir." After the detective sat down, the room grew quiet as they both felt uncomfortable around each other again. "So, where is your wife? She still is your wife right." He asked raising his brow.

"Yes sir. That's right."

"Then why was she acting as Ted's wife at the funeral."

"Well, that's a long story."

"So I guess that's why you were at the funeral. Man, you didn't waist any time getting your wife back did you?" _____ "You know if I didn't know any better it don't sound like Ted died by accident."

"Well in that case it sounds like I am going to need my lawyer." Mr. Johnson responded sarcastically but seriously.

"Ok, ok, no need to get all lawyered up on me now."

Suddendly, Mrs. Johnson walks in fully dressed with a skirt and blouse on.

The detective acknowledges her by turning around and giving her a nod. He turns the note on his pad as he had when he walked in. "Well I have one question for her before you get all lawyer up on me." He said turning back around to Mr. Johnson then back at Mrs. Johnson. "Tell me this, if you were his wife then where was Ted staying?"

"He had a place across town somewhere." Mr. Johnson answered quickly.

The detective looks at Mrs. Johnson to confirm what Mr. Johnson said. She nods.

"Mrs. Johnson do you know you can be fined for being married to two men at the same time?"

"Uuh, I will take care of the fine. Are you finished?" Mr. Johnson asked leaning forward to give a stronger presence.

"Yes, I will be back."

"Make sure you come back with my lawyer."

"I heard that before," he thought motioning his head and slightly grinning.

He drives to the house where Ted had gotten shot. As he was pulling up to the house, he noticed a mailman putting mail in their box.

"Here, can I see that mail before you put it in that box?" Detective Mac asked climbing out of his car and showing the mailman his badge.

As he goes through the mail, he runs across a moving bill addressed to Mrs. Felicia Johnson from Davis Movers. *Davis Movers, I will be giving them a call,"* he thought. "Hey do you get mail from a Ted Humphrey to be sent here." The detective asked as he looked up at the mailman.

"I think I get some job applications but I can't remember any bills or anything like that. Who is he anyway and what is he to Mr. Johnson? And is Mrs. Johnson last name still Johnson? The mail man asked the detective hoping he can clear up some confusion from their incoming mail.

"Well it's a long story but I think she still goes by that name."

"It's been some crazy things going on there every since their son died."

"Yeah, I believe it's about to get crazier." The detective responded with a hint of concern.

Another Thought

Back in the hotel Mrs. Johnson sits on the couch thinking about whether are not she is interested in going through this again. She also has thoughts of Ted. Mr. Johnson leans beside her and is hugging her. As he is hugging her and glad to have her back, he keeps thinking about the doctor's comment of her being with another man. But he holds those thoughts in for now. His only concern now is getting back control of his woman.

A thought of Fred suddenly pops in Mrs. Johnson's head.

"Oh Ted. Mr. Johnson suddenly snaps away from her and looks at her expressionless. "I am sorry, but we got to go pick up Fred."

"Alright, I will drive." said Mr. Johnson softly biting his lips with irritation in his eyes.

Mrs. Johnson grabs her things and Mr. Johnson puts his jacket on and they both walk out the hotel door. Mrs. Johnson stops to turn around the do not disturb sign to read please clean.

When they got in the car, Mrs. Johnson had a curious question lingering in her mind.

"So Mister, can you explain something to me?"

She never calls him Mister unless she was serious about something.

"Like what?" Mr. Johnson asked letting out some air still not convinced that her apology was sincere enough for him to forget what she said.

"Well that gun that they showed that shot"… she thought not to say his name again. "You know.

Mr. Johnson slightly nods.

"That wasn't our gun, right?"

"Yeah." Mr. Johnson answered softly avoiding eye contact.

"So, whose gun was it and," she suddenly stops the flow and gets another thought. "You know what, I always take the bullets out the gun and put them somewhere else so I don't think our gun was even loaded so Fred couldn't have done that."

Mr. Johnson smiles slightly and never takes his eyes off the road to look at Mrs. Johnson's expression.

"You are covering for somebody aren't you? I hope it's not that doctor." she said rolling her eyes as she turns her head momentarily. "So, you got that little boy walking around thinking that he killed Ted. You should be ashamed of yourself." She exclaimed folding her arms.

"Well if Fred didn't kill him, I would have. Anyway, don't go back and tell Fred or the cops. Because, if they find out they will go after me and then the family will be separated again. Don't you think we've been through enough already." He finally momentarily turns his head to look at Mrs. Johnson as he pulled up to a stop light. "Besides, Fred appears to be handling it well that he shot that man. He met a cool role model, Brent too. Come on, can we be a family again?" It was quiet for fifteen seconds. "And lets not bring that man up again, alright." He adds with a quick glance at Mrs. Johnson before pulling off to get on the highway.

"Alright. But you know that detective is not going to give up on this, right."

"Honey, our tracks are being covered, I am not going to be the one to separate us again.

"Oh, you going to fix this, huh?" asked Mrs. Johnson expressionless.

"Yeah, hopefully." he responded hoping that the doctor will take care of the detective.

They pulled up in front of Ms. Byrd's house.

Mrs. Johnson grew curious. "How did you know where Ms. Byrd stayed? I never remembered bringing you over here with me." she asked turning her head to see him give his answer.

"Uh, uh." he utters because he don't want to blow Trish's cover. "Girl you know I got connections. Come on, lets go get the boy." Mr. Johnson said while quickly grabbing the latch on the door and quickly stepping out of the car to avoid that subject.

Mrs. Johnson's mouth goes to the left in disbelief.

As they walked to the door, they can see Brent and Fred playing a game on the television. They knock and Brent quickly put the game on pause. He gets to the door and smiles at Mrs. Johnson and frowns at Mr. Johnson.

"What was that for?" Mrs. Johnson asked noticing the frown at her husband. "What? You all know each other?"

Mr. Johnson looks down and smirks.

"First, you know where Ms. Byrd stays and now you are going to tell me that you and her son are acquaintances." she asked raising her brow.

Mr. Johnson lifts his head, shrugs his shoulders and grins.

"Hey mama what's up?" Fred said while staring at Mrs. Johnson and not really acknowledging Mr. Johnson.

"Oh, I guess you aren't talking to me either," said Mr. Johnson looking at Brent to see if he may have said something about his involvement with the killing of his daddy. "I suggest you give me a hug so we can start all over as a family again, unless you want to go back to one of those homes." He looks at Fred with one eye wider than the other one.

Fred looks at Brent to get his confirmation. Mr. Johnson notices that and was uncomfortable.

Brent nods.

Fred gives him a hand shake and Mr. Johnson pulls him in to hug him. "Yeah, we are a family again. Things happen for a reason. So don't take nothing you did out of context. Just like the preacher said at my son's funeral. There is nothing I could have done, you could have done or we could have done. In God's eyes it had to happen." said Mr. Johnson as he waves Mrs. Johnson to hug her along with Fred.

Mrs. Johnson smiles at the sound of God coming out of her husband's mouth. So did Ms. Byrd who had walked right beside her.

"You'll want some breakfast?" asked Ms. Byrd still carrying her smile.

"No Ms. Byrd we are going to grab something on the way back home. We got a lot of catching up to do and sitting down having breakfast somewhere will be great."

"Oh, I bet." Ms. Byrd said with a smile. Look at you, you went and got your woman. She said with a proud gleam on her face.

"So you two been talking or something?" Mrs. Johnson asked pointing at both of them looking embarrass from Ms. Byrd's comment.

"Yeah, remember when I told you about what happened at the store?"

"Oh yeah, that's right. Here, can Fred take these clothes and go get washed up before we head back out."

"He sure can, I am sure he knows where the bathroom is because he lit it up earlier. Once I saw that shake from McDonald's in the kitchen trash, I knew what did it." he said with a smile as Fred walked by her avoiding eye contact and wearing a slight grin on his face.

"Hey Brent let's talk man to man outside on the porch and let these two have that woman to woman talk while we wait on Fred." asked Mr. Johnson changing the tone.

As they walked outside the door, Mr. Johnson continues to give Brent a hard stare.

"Brent what did you tell Fred?" Mr. Johnson asked in a low but angry tone.

"I didn't tell him anything."

"Why was he acting like that?"

"Man, what you expect, you been missing for two years and come back as if someone supposed to feel the same about you."

"Yeah, I guess you right. But why did he look at you a few minutes ago like you are his father?"

"Brother, he don't know who's his father is now. I think you are just over exaggerating."

"Alright, let me find out you told him." said Mr. Johnson biting his lips.

"Uh, I think you are forgetting who is the hitman." he reminded him with one eye raised.

"I am just saying"…….. .

Brent's cell phone rings interrupting their conversation.

"Hold that thought." Brent asked holding one finger in the air. He looks to see whose calling; it's the doctor. "See, this is a customer right here, excuse me." Brent said while walking off the porch to get more privacy.

"I thought he was not doing that anymore." Mr. Johnson thought.

Moments later Fred comes running out the door onto the porch.

He sees Mr. Johnson but not Brent.

"Where Brent go?" he asked anxiously.

Mr. Johnson pointed outside.

Fred hurries off the porch with no hesitation.

"Hey Brent"……….he yells with a smile.

Brent put one finger up to ask Fred to hold that thought. He writes information down on a piece of paper.

While Brent is on the phone, Mrs. Johnson walks out the door with Ms. Byrd.

"Honey are you ready?" Mrs. Johnson asked Mr. Johnson and Fred answered at the same time.

"Oh, well I guess I got to get used to this again." replied Mr. Johnson with a glance at Fred.

Brent, who is still on the phone gives dap to Fred with his free hand.

Moments later Curtis comes out of his room. "Did I hear the young man leave?"

"Yeah, what you doing out here? Boy get back in there before you get your cold back." Ms. Byrd brushed Curtis back in and looks out a window and sees Brent was still on the phone talking to the doctor. "That must be a really important call, he hasn't budged from that phone."

"He's probably back selling." Curtis said abruptly.

"Boy why would you say something like that, you need to give your brother a chance just like I am."

"Ok mom, he's not going to do nothing but let you down, mark my words."

"Well, mark my words when he takes his drug selling skills and uses it for selling something legal. You know it won't surprise me if he is trying to make a deal now." Ms. Byrd said trying her best to think positive for Brent and trying to get her son to do the same.

She looks out the window and sees Brent still on the phone.

I Promise I Won't Let You Down

As Brent talks on his cell phone, he noticed Ms. Byrd looking out at him through the window at him. He turns to sit inside his car.

"Hey man, just do your job and take care of your debt. Now do it exactly how I asked you, alright." The doctor demanded on the other end.

"Alright doctor, I promise I won't let you down this time. But you are going to have to pay me something to pay my people." Brent said back into the phone.

"Will you just do what I say? I got whatever they need. I think Mr. Johnson can help me out too."

"O, the rich cat, huh?"

"Whatever, just follow the plan and everything is going to work out. Now let me get off here so I can make another phone call."

"Oh, wait a minute before you do that, I think he is having a make up dinner with his wife and son now."

"Boy, do you really think I care! How do you know that anyway?"

"Because, Fred and both of the Johnson's just left my mother's house."

"What! You know"… The doctor takes in some breath and lets it out. "Never mind, just try to get the detective to meet you at the store after it closes alright. You going to make sure your man know what to do right?"

"Yeah he will be cool."

"Now remember it must look like a robbery gone bad."

"I got this, okay. You make sure you got my money."

"Is he a good shooter?"

"Don't worry. I am getting ready to make a call for that now."

"Alright, because you know I will have to take care of you if you don't have me money right."

"Brent, we discussed this when we was locked up together. So please don't talk to me like a child."

"I am just saying, I am going out the way with this murder because the detective is kinda of cool because he use too hook up my boy Ted, Ted never went to jail because of him I think. I suppose to be out of this business." Brent said then he pauses.

" Brent but I told you that Ted was working with the cops anyway in jail remember."

"Yeah, but I thought you was just lying because we both had had our ends with him."

"Alright, but we got to hurry. So let me make this call to get some help with your money. We will be in touch."

Will You Just Turn That Off

Mr. and Mrs. Johnson and Fred are chatting as they wait for the waitress to bring their order. As they are chatting, Mr. Johnson's phone rings suddenly.

"Hello." he answered.

"Will you just turn that off for one hour? We are trying to have a special breakfast." Mrs. Johnson ordered in an angry tone.

"Just wait one second." He said putting one finger in the air.

"Hello." the man said on the other end.

"So, you and Brent are good friends now, huh?"

At that moment a waiter approaches them handing them their food. Mr. Johnson moves back and allows the waitress to set his plate in front of him on the table as he never loses concentration of the phone conversation.

"What? Doctor, just get to the reason for this phone call, what's up?"

"Well, you want me to be out of your hair again right."

"Hell, yeah, I am trying to get my family back together!"

"Right. So I need you to do something for me."

"No. I got my family back and I am not going to mess it back up with you." he said putting his head down to talk in a low tone and trying not to let Mrs. Johnson hear the whole conversation.

Mrs. Johnson moves her arm down swiftly as if she was hanging up a make believe phone hoping that he will get the point.

"Lets make another agreement?" Dr. Cashion asked hoping it will influence him to help.

"As far as I am concerned the agreement days are over. It's like this doc, when we made that first agreement it was like a book and the book showed that I will do anything for my son. This is currently a new book of my life. And this book will show that I am a man trying to get his family back." he proudly said looking up at Mrs. Johnson and Fred to confirm his statement. He stops and just stares at Mrs. Johnson who is looking at him disgusted.

"Ok this will be the last time, alright. You want the detective off our case right?"

Mr. Johnson fills his jaw up with air and releases it. "What are you planning on doing this time?" he asked in an agitated tone.

"Uh, I think I got a plan and when it works, you will be able to start a family like you want."

"Alright doc, what you need me to do?" he asked picking up a piece of sausage off his plate and getting up from the table and walking towards the restaurant's bathrooms.

"It's a long story but can you just meet me at the Barry's Bank later?"

"What?" Mr. Johnson asked to make sure he heard the doctor right.

"Yeah, Barry's Bank. You know where that is Mr. Money." said the doctor.

"Yeah.Yeah."

"Just meet me there tomorrow at 3:30p.m. in the morning and I will share the details with you then. Now get back to your wife before she leaves you again." He said playfully.

Mr. Johnson didn't take it seriously so he quickly closes the flap on his phone and takes quick steps back to his seat. When he gets in eye sight, he noticed Mrs. Johnson and Fred eating silent without expression.

"So is the food good?" Mr. Johnson asked as soon as he approached the table.

"What?" Mrs. Johnson utters because she was surprised that Mr. Johnson came back to the table like nothing happened. "Dude what was that all about?"

"Nothing really, he just need a favor?" he said as he lifts another piece of sausage in his mouth.

"Ok, what did he need?" she asked with one eye wider.

Meanwhile, the doctor sits in a motel room and thinks about the detective and the plan as he prepares to use some drugs he had bought from the streets earlier.

He sees the drugs he bought on a table. It reminded him of the day after the graduation when his two friends left those drugs on the table and later he tries them for the first time.

"I miss you " he jokingly said to the drugs as they laid on the table and smiles.

The Planning Stages

Later, Mr. Johnson and the doctor meets. "Alright, you understand what I need for you to do right." The doctor asked Mr. Johnson who stares off as if he is in a daze. When he never replies, the doctor grows angry. "Listen now, don't act like I never did nothing I didn't want to do for you."

Mr. Johnson turns his head to meet his eyes. "How long are you going to keep bringing that up?" he asked with irritated eyes.

"Until my life is back together!" Dr. Cashion expresses with determination. "I tell you after that handshake, my life has never been the same." the doctor said with a smirk. "So, are you going to do it or what?"

"What's in it for me?"

"Me being out of your hair. I know how important it is for you to get back with your family and if you do it for me, then I promise to not bother you ever again. Otherwise I am going to be calling you and showing up at your doorstep and I know you don't want that seeing how your wife feels about me. So take my advice and help me get rid of the detective."

The doctor knew exactly where to hit Mr. Johnson to get him to do what he asked. "So all I have to do is give you this money and you promise to stay out of my life."

"Right. That's all." he said with a half smile.

Mr. Johnson just moves his head expressionless.

The Phone Clicks

The detective just arrived at work to investigate the incident at the house. He is trying to understand Mrs. Johnson and Ted's relationship.

He calls the movers.

"Hello! Davis Movers, the company that moves when you move." a worker said when he answers the phone.

"Hello, this is Detective Mac and I am investigating a recent customer of yours. Do you remember moving something for the Humphrey's?"

"Hold on, let me check my files." the worker answered as he gets up from the chair he was sitting in and walking to the file cabinet. "OK, I do have a Ted Humphrey. Did we do something wrong?"

"No, no, no, I am just trying to clear up some things."

"Well the movers said that the house looked like a crime just happened there. I thought that was strange."

"What? You guys don't know what happen to him?" asked the Detective because he thought it was big news in the neighborhood.

"No, the movers don't bother to ask questions, they are there to do a job. For all we knew she may be going through a nasty divorce."

"Well, he was shot."

"What! My driver thought something was going on that day because when they showed up the first time, there was a lot of cops around the house……. So he was murdered, huh?

"Yeah, if you wanna say that." responded Detective Mac ready to get off the phone.

"Do they have a suspect?"

"Maybe, but I have to go. Thank you for your information. Contact the station if you get any more information." The detective asked before he clicks over to answer another call.

"Detective Mac." he answered the other line.

"Hello, What's up man?"

"What's going on? Who is this?" asked the detective curiously.

"This is Brent and I got some information about Dr. Cashion that will put him in jail for life this time."

"Oh yeah, what you got?"

"I have to give it to you. It's some real strong evidence that shows that he is the one that did this to you."

"Oh yeah, why are you trying to do this for me? I mean, what's in it for you?"

"Why are you asking all these questions? Do you want the information or what? Well, I just don't like the doctor too and feel he needs to pay for the things I know he done. I wrote everything down he told me he done in jail." Brent said with proudness.

"So why you do that? That's unusual don't you think."

"I was going to use it against him if I had too." He thought I was his friend and he still thinks I am his friend, but he must know that even lock up everybody is for themselves.

"Oh, alright, what you got?" he asked with a hint of being impatient.

"Hold up, you know nothing is for free. Meet me at the grocery store."

"I knew you wanted something." he mumbled."Which one?"

"Rich Groceries off of King Street. I gonna need about $5000.00 for this information."

"For real? I will check our witness funds." he asked remembering that's where they arrested the doctor.

"Yeah a little bit after it closes. Around 11:00p.m."

"Oh alright, alright. In the parking lot I guess?"

"Yeah, you must know something about that spot huh?" Brent asked with a hint of suspicious.

"Yeah, I actually grew up in that area. I know that's like the middle ground where people meet at now to do all their dirty work now right?

"Right, you know what's up? I guess." he said as he is ending the conversation. "See you at 11:00p.m. Call me if you get there before I do."

"I am not going to stay long if you are not there? Hell, I will tell somebody to come with me but this is personal, I will hate one of my officers to get hurt if something goes down on my personal business. So I hope this is some legit stuff but I am not too worried because I got people on the pay roll from the area. It's kind of where I grew up at. You hear me."

"I will be there on time. I just said that in case you decide to get there earlier. Call me if you gonna be late too."

"Alright, Mr. Byrd. Thank you for helping me alright."

The phone disconnects.

Your Brother is on the Phone

" Rich Groceries." answers the store's clerk Trish.

"Hello, yeah, this Brent let me speak to my brother."

"Hold on." Trish presses the hold button and notices the manager near her in one of the isles.

"Mr. Byrd, your brother wants to speak to you." She informed him in a loud enough tone for him to hear.

"Aye, asked him can I call him back." he yells while counting some cans.

"He said can he call you back?" Trish asked the caller as she starts ringing out a customer who just walked to her register.

"No, this can't wait, tell him it's an emergency."

"Mr. Byrd, he said it's an emergency." she said raising her voice. "That will be $24.09. she informed a customer as she lowered her voice to a more pleasant tone."

"Alright, put him on hold, I am going to take it in the back." her boss said as he climbs down a stool and walks to the back storage area to the managers' office.

"Hello, this is the manager Mr. Byrd." he said as soon as he picked up the phone on the desk.

"Hello, this is the manager Mr. Byrd." Brent marks him. "Man this is your brother. Answer the phone like you know next time."

"Ok, you right, I am just use to always answering the phone like that. I am not thinking. What's up? What's the emergency?"

"Huh, are you going to be out there in time tonight?"

"I guess we are trying too, if we don't get a lot of last minutes customers and my brother lets me get off this phone so I can finish counting my stock." he sarcastically replies. "But why you want to know?"

"I just heard some gangs are going to meet on the parking lot there and there's no telling what's going to happen."

"Oh yeah? Where did you hear that?"

"In the streets! Where else? You just make sure you are out. I think they are coming right after the store closes."

"Ah right. Ah right. Good looking out brother. I knew God will find some way to use your street knowledge to help out the better man."

"Oh, so why you think you are the better man, because momma favored you?"

"No. I meant to say better mankind. But momma didn't favor me, more then she favored you."

"She just felt you needed more hard discipline then I did because of some of the choices you were making growing up. You know what I mean. I mean it's like this brother, I heard a preacher talk about this. He said something like God created us all differently, so what makes you think that we all should be raised the same. That's what momma did."

"Man whatever, if momma could have treated me as half as good as she treated you, I would be in a better position now."

"Brother if mom would have been as discipline to me as she was on you, I probably be running for President now." he said not allowing his brother to use mom as an excuse for his actions.

"Man whatever, I was always on some type of punishment when I was growing up. All I remember is you playing outside and I am in the house most of the time."

"Man I got on punishment too. But I can admit, you were on punishment a lot more than me. I think momma was just trying to get you to be able to make better choices. But I guess it didn't work out."

"See!" He bites his lip and lets out some wind. "Brother, outside of that last remark, I see where you coming from."

"Good. But look brother, I got to get off this phone and finish my counts so I can get out of here in time before those gangs show up."

"Right. I am up too. Bro man I am really going to be thinking about what you said about making better choices. Alright."

"Alright, you promise."

"Man yeah. Hell mom made me promise about that too. Bro get out of there before they start shooting."

"Okay, bro peace." he saluted as he looks at the security camera and realizes it's out of tape. *"Ah man I better get another tape because I know the cops will ask for it if something goes down."* he thought.

131

"Trish, my brother just told me that some gangs are about to meet here and there's no telling what's about to go down."

"OK." Trish replied picking up her jacket that was hanging over her stool in front of the cash register.

The Set-up

Brent sits in his car as he made it to the store before the detective. He calls Russ to reenact the plan.

"So you know what to do right?"

"Yeah, I am ready." He replied sitting on a bus stop bench.

"Now don't even wait for him to get out the car. Just go for it as soon as he pulls up beside me, alright your money should be on him or in the car, you going to take, bet?"

"Bet that. You ain't said nothing but a word. I am high too." Russ said as he is eager to do the job too get money.

"You high? What you get high for? You didn't spend all the money I gave you on weed did you?"

"Brent man, I can't do this in a normal mind. Nah I didn't. Now stop asking me questions, you blowing my high!" he said as he takes another hit.

"Man, just don't fuck up."

"I am not. I'm not." He said twice taking another puff.

Brent sits in the car as he waits patiently for the detective to arrive. He turns on his CD and plays his jam. He beats the stirring wheel with his thumb as he raps with the rapper that's rapping to his song. Minutes go by and from a distance he sees a car pulling up in front of the store through his review mirror. The car stops and then drives slowly towards Brent's car. Brent puts his head down as he doesn't want to see what's about to happen to the detective. He thinks about his life and what his brother said about how and why mom was that way.

As he hears the car approaching him he hopes that Russ does his business before he has to establish I contact with him. The car blows his horn and Brent sees Russ looking from his peripheral vision. He still hears the release of a bullet come out of a silencer the shooter had. Brent waste no time to leave the parking lot as he only hopes that everything works out. He drives to his mother house and waits on his brother.

He gets a phone call and it's Russ.

"Aye, I did it. What's up with that money?" he asked looking around the car.

"Man he didn't have it on him or in the ride?" asked Brent.

Russ glances in the back seat and sees a bag.

"O, alright. I guess it's back here in this bag. I see something in the back seat. I'll let you know when I get far away from the crime. See you partner."

"Man. Don't call me that. I just had a discussion with my brother about changing by life. This will be the last time I do something like this."

"Ah man, you still talking that mess. When are you going to admit you are nothing but a career criminal. Call me when you get another job."

"Man, I am serious." His phone clicks and he sees that it's his brother. "Here is my brother now. Let me go so I can talk to him."

Brent clicks over but the call suddenly disconnects.

"Hello, hello!" he said into the phone not hearing his brother's reply.

"Man he must had click over to one of his gals. Let me call him back." Right at that time the television in the front room announces a news flash at the Grocery Store.

He puts the phone back down and away from his ear.

"This just in, there has been another shooting at Rich Groceries and there appears to be fatality. It's speculated that the victim either got caught up in the cross fire of a gang war or he was carjack. Detective will be checking the store surveillance for more evidence soon. Again we are at Rich Groceries and apparently a man, we will tell you his gender and that's all we can tell right now and don't know if you all remember but a years ago there was a shooting inside the store, when a man was looking for his wife was shoot by officers. Wow, anyway, anyone with information on this current incident, please contact the police department at the number on the screen." announced a news reporter.

Gradually, Ms. Byrd walks in holding a plate that she had fix for her son.

"What was that about?" she asked only hearing the news reporter last statement.

Brent picks up the remote and changes the station not wanting to get her excited over nothing.

"Nothing, some kids still acting stupid."

"Look who's talking. You still in the streets probably still selling drugs as far as I know."

"I hope not. I thought jail was teaching you a little humanity. Especially when you found that doctor to help me with my heart condition. I said to myself I must had instill something in you right." She looks at him with a proud look on her face.

Brent looks back and offers a half smile from the comment he sees the plate in her hands. "Is that for me?" he asked.

"No, this is for your brother, he normally comes by around this time and I want to make sure I had a plate for him ready and hot."

"You never had a plate for me ready and hot?" Brent asked lifting his head to the side and raising his brow.

"I know, that's because I never know when you are coming. I mean the only time I knew you were coming is when you had got out of prison. Your brother is routine, he will get off work and be here around 11:30pm. Although he kind of late now but he called me earlier and told me that he will be a little late because he had to take his coworker home and stop by the store to get a video tape or something."

"Oh that's why huh?"

"Yeah, what else you think?"

"I thought you love him better than me. I mean you always treated him better than me."

"That's because you were hard headed. I always catch your brother doing good things but I knew that you was up to something even if I ever caught you doing the right thing. I guess I could had gave you the benefit of the doubt but you push me to think that way and if you think I was a little harder on you, then I am sorry but that still don't give you an excuse to be the way you are. You had choices and I know life history gave you the option on where each will go. You chose the wrong path, the path that will lead you to either death or jail. You already been to jail." A brief moment of silence as she looks at him with wonder in her eyes. I just hope you are on the right path now because I don't want to see you die knowing what you could had accomplished in this life time."

Suddenly, Brent's cell phone rings.

His mother scratches her throat.

"I have to take this." He said to her as he glances to his phone and back to her. He turns to going outside on the porch.

"Brent you haven't changed. I will appreciate it if you don't come back until you do, ok."

"Hold up, momma. I got to go." He said opening the door and letting himself out on the porch.

"What's up Bro? You not still at the store?" he asked knowing the answer already.

"No Brent. Where are you?"

"Who is this?"

"So, I guess that bullet was meant for me, huh?" the detective asked biting his lips.

"I don't know what you are talking about? Where is my brother?"

"Well your brother has been shot."

"Nooo! Hell no! O my Gawd! Is he dead?"

"Brent, The ambulance emergency technicians has taken him to the hospital. So if you were on your way here, just meet us at the hospital."

Brent checks his pockets and realizes he left his keys in the house. Now he has to go back in try to avoid any eye contact with his mother.

When Brent walks in the house, he notices his mother standing there in a daze, when he saw his keys and reach for them, he notice the plate that was in his mother's hand was on the floor now.

He stared down at the plate and slowly guides his eyes to meet his mother's eyes which were in a daze as she looks frozen.

"You alright?" he wondered as he stood up to guide his eyes to where she is staring at.

"We are back again with some more on that shooting it looks as if it was a car jack. Neighbor say that he had just purchase a brand new car. Wow, I guess it don't pay to have nice stuff these days."

In no time, a knock was at the door. Brent looks at his mother who looks as if she is about to faint.

He grabs her and drags her to the couch. Suddenly the knock came again.

"Knock, knock, knock."

"Who is it?" asked Brent making sure his mother was comfortiable before getting the door.

"It's Officer Grinstin. I need to speak to an adult of the Byrds."

"No, no, no!" Ms. Byrd yelled repeatedly in sorrow.

"Can I come in?" asked the officer.

"Yeah, the door is open." He yelled.

When the officer walks in, he see Brent on the couch with his arm around his mother. He then looks at the television and sees that it's on the news.

"Oh, I guess I am late, huh."

"Do we already know what happen?"

'Brent looks at the officer with a blank stare as he continues to hold his arm around his mother.

"Anybody needs a ride to the hospital to identify the body."

Ms, Byrd lets out another loud cry and boiled up inside.

"Man get out, I got a car. Thank you."

"Don't worry, we got some keys to the store we are going to check the vedio to find this killer and anybody associate with him.

Brent nods and he never looks into the officer's eyes again.

The officer exits the house to his squad car. He notifies the unit on his radio that the parents been notified.

Brent and his mother arrived at the hospital. They abruptly gets held back by emergency hospital security. After a brief struggle, they sit down in the waiting room.

"Son just talk to me. Did you have anything to do with your brother's death?" asked his mother calming down.

"No mama, I didn't. I swear." He said looking her in the eye to make sure that she believes him.

"Boy don't, swear to me. Son don't take this the wrong way, but I had prepared myself for this phone call about you but I am nowhere prepared for this."

"Silence between the two as the background noise fills the room with television, babies crying, receptionist taking care of business and so on.

A man walks over to them wearing a white lab jacket. "Are you the Byrd's.

They both look up at him with wet eyes and nods.

"Come with me."

They walked to the elevator and down to the morge and when they saw the body, the both broke down in sorrow.

Moments later an officer came by and they followed the officer to the station. Brent agreed to go with them because he didn't want his mother to get suspicious that he had something to do with his death.

News Flash

"Where is that boy!" shouted the doctor when he hears Brent's voice mail. "It's hard to find good help these days." he continued.

He then picks up the phone and calls Mr. Johnson.

"Hello." answered Mr. Johnson after three rings.

"Hello, I think Brent let me down." he replied in a soft tone.

"What do you mean?"

"Well, he's not answering his phone."

"Oh well." he hears something on the TV. "Sh!sh!sh!"

"This just in, a manager at a local Grocery store was shot after what appears to be a car jack. He is being seen at the hospital. No word on his condition. We will give you more information as it develops." announced the news anchor.

"Hey Doctor, they just said on the news a manager at a grocery store was just shot during a car jack. Do you think that was your thing?"

"They didn't give no names or nothing?"

"No, it was a news flash."

"Hey, call me back when you see the news."

"Well doc, he suddenly stops the conversation because the story suddenly pops back on the news. "Hey I will call you back, it's back on."

"Wait, can you put the phone to the speaker."

Mr. Johnson does exactly what the doctor requested for him to do and afterwards the news anchor begins to talk.

"That was Rich Groceries. Witnesses say that around closing time someone car jacked a manager and he was shot. Again no word of his condition."

Silence as both of them are mesmerized by the story.

"This has gone too far again." Mr. Johnson said under his breath breaking the silence.

"Yes. I know."

Mrs. Johnson walks in the room where Mr. Johnson is talking on the phone. He looks down and away to avoid eye contact with her. Mrs. Johnson starts reaching for the phone to hang it up. Mr. Johnson pushes her reaching arm away from him.

"Hello Doctor I have to go, my wife is losing it!" he said with irritated eyes.

"That's right doctor we don't need your service anymore. Leave us alone!" Mrs. Johnson exclaimed in her loudest voice to make sure the doctor hears her.

Mr. Johnson hangs up the phone and looks immensely at Mrs. Johnson. "Everything is going to be alright." said Mr. Johnson as he was thinking about the incident just happened at the store and is glad he has nothing to do with it.

Mrs. Johnson tips her head back and grabs Mr. Johnson's biceps to push herself away. "Please don't try to fix this. This is how all this started. You was trying to fix our son." Mrs. Johnson said looking Mr. Johnson directly in the eyes.

Mr. Johnson couldn't say a word. He just looked at her without expression.

Next to no time, Fred walks in the room and sees Mrs. Johnson upset. Fred gets upset because she was so happy when she got with Ted. Now she's back to this difficult man. "*Something must be done*," he thought as he stares at Mr. Johnson without an expression. Mr. Johnson notice him and briefly established eye contact and Fred looked away and walked back to the other room.

"You know, this may be a bad time to talk about this but I think we are going to have to give Fred back to a home." Mr. Johnson said still looking in the direction of Fred.

"Oh no, no you don't. If anything you will go back to a home." Mrs. Johnson replied folding her arms.

"No, honey I am just saying he's not the same, he's been acting strange."

"Well, how does a 13 year old boy supposed to act after all he has been through? He has also just been accused for killing his father, I mean stepfather. I am still kind of puzzled about that because that wasn't your gun and I believe I heard the doctor in here the day it happened."

Mr. Johnson continued to look in Fred's direction never turning to acknowledge Mrs. Johnson's statement.

"Fred needs to know the truth, if he didn't do that." Mrs. Johnson continued as she gives Mr. Johnson a penetrating stare to try to get him to feel her stare.

He turns to her to look at her back with a raised eye brow.

The Next Day

When the detective walks out into the garage, he decides to call Brent.

"Yeah." Brent said softly when he answered the phone noticing it's the detective.

"So, I guess you are still down, huh." asked the detective staring at the bullet on the desk in front of him.

"Yeah, but I am mainly down for my mother."

"Ah yeah, I know she is taking it hard too. I betcha he was considered the good son want he."

"Yep he sure was but hell what's up?"

"But tell me was that just a coincidence that your brother got car jack on the same day and time we were suppose to meet?"

"Uh, yeah? That's all it was."

"O, was it also a coincidence that all the videos where out in the store too?"

"I don't know I guess." He gets a little more confidence that his brother's death want get trace back to him.

"So before I ask you this, do you know who might have done this to you brother?

"Naw but he going to get what's coming him."

The conversation came to a complete halt as Brent takes in the fact that his brother was shot by Russ.

"Man I hope you just let the police handle their jobs, alright. No need to get your mother all upset again. This should be a wake up call for you to get your life together. But anyway, you still got information to give me to get the doctor?"

"I don't know!" Brent said as he feels the doctor had a lot to do with his brother being dead. Brent swallows as he sees where the dectective is coming from but not enough to not want to still kill Russ. "You want to get the doctor for real?"

"That's right."

"Well how about if you act like you are………."

"No, don't even go where I think you are getting ready to go with this." the detective rebutts before he finished explaining. "We already tried what I think you are getting ready to say and I know the doctor is not going to fall for that twice."

"Oh, you did try to set him up like that. He told me something like that when we were locked up together."

"Yeah, he helped my moms out, so I promised to help him out."

"Oh, how did he help your mother, again?"

"Well, I told him what was going on with my mother's heart and how the doctor acted as if they didn't know how to help her. So he had me to tell them to check this part on her and they did and that was it. My moms felt a lot different about me then."

"What dumb doctor was this? So I won't go to him?"

"The neighborhood crooked doctor, Dr. Saviss. A brief silence as the detective never responds as he closes the door and locks it to return back to the station.

"You know the doctor looked weird when I told him who this doctor was. He had a smirky look on his face."

"What's his name again?" Detective Mac asked moving stuff away from his desk to find his pad to write his name down.

"Dr. Saviss, why? Do you think you know him?"

"No, no, I am just taking notes. But ain't that the doctor who be taking whatever he can to get people to pay before he do anything to help him. I remember one time he took the guys drugs when he told him he will pay when he sell out. He took the drugs and said he will just sell them himself. I mean he do anything to make sure people pay off their debt but nobody touches him. I guess because they think he is a broke doctor trying to help the people."

"Yeah anyway, I call will call you back when I get a plan together." Brent said hearing someone at the door.

"Alright." the detective replies.

Brent walks to the door and welcome the visitors who are really coming to see Mrs. Byrd and Brent can feel the negative vibe from the visitors who are suspicious of Brent's involvements with his brother's death.

Do You Know a Dr. Cashion

After the detective hangs up the phone, he grabs the book to look up the doctor him and Brent just spoke of. He finds the doctor in the yellow pages.

"Hello." a nurse answered when he picked up the phone to make his call.

"Hello, this is the detective from Barry County. Is there a Dr. Saviss there?"

"Yes, who are you again?"

"Detective Mac from Barry County."

"Oh, alright as soon as he..." it dawns on her where she knows this detective from. "I tell you what, can you hold? I will see where he's at with this patient."

"Oh, you can have him to call me back."

"Well, I'll just go see where he's at with the patient. She just came in for a checkup." She pushes the hold button on the phone and walks back in the room where the doctor is talking to a patient.

"I tell you doctor if I find out that my son had something to do with his death, I will be in your office again."

"Well, he seems like a good person. I mean he did help me discover what was wrong with you."

"Whatever."

"Knock, knock, knock." The nurse is knocking on the doctor's door.

"Doctor you have someone who needs to talk to you. It's a detective and it sounds important."

"OK Mrs. Byrd, you get it together and in the meantime, the nurse will be in to give you your prescription."

The doctor walks back with the nurse and as soon as he got out of ear shot from Ms. Byrd. He asked the nurse. "What kind of doctor am I?"

"Uh Internal, I guess?"

"Right, I am not a psychologist. So why does that woman think I need to hear about all her life issues?"

The nurse shruggs her shoulders with a half smile. "Here, it's a detective, she whispers handing him the phone.

The doctor takes it with concern in his eyes.

"Hello, this is Dr. Saviss. How may I help you?"

"Hello, Dr. Saviss. I didn't catch you at a bad time did I?"

"Actually, you couldn't be more prompt." the doctor replied thinking about how Ms. Byrd was talking him to death. "So, what's up detective?"

"Here's what's up Doctor? I am going to get right down to it. Do you know a Dr. Cashion?"

"Who!" His attitude completely changes when he hears that name.

Ms. Byrd comes out the back and the nurse hands her samples. "Here, just take theses and here's the prescription. I hope everything works out for you."

"Baby, I got the Lord on my side, so I know everything is going to work out for me." She says while grabbing her things. "Bye doctor." she yelled seeing Brent coming in the door to pick her up.

"Hold on." asked the doctor putting his hand over the receiver. "OK, Mrs. Byrd, you come back and see me if it goes back up." After a nod to Mrs. Byrd, he turns and looks at the nurse. "Hey I am going to take this in my office. Put this on hold. I will pick it up when I get back into my office."

The Doctor walks back in his office and closes the door behind him. When the nurse sees the hold button stops flashing she picks up the phone to ease drop on the doctor and the detective's conversation.

"Yes, I am back. Now did you say a Dr Cashion? asked Dr. Saviss taking his seat.

"Yes. Do you know him?"

"Yeah I know him. When that news came out on him, one of my classmates contacted me feeling a little remorseful. Then he told me something that he did to me at school."

"Oh yeah, what he do?"

"Lets just say he made me fail a serious project and I was in turmoil for ages. In fact, I had to admit myself in the hospital after going through a long depression."

"Oh, wow." Detective Mac said wondering how someone could be so evil.

"Is he back in town?" he asked checking the drawer where he keeps his gun at because he works in a high crime area.

"Yeah, but I don't know where. That's why I am calling you."

"Well, I can't tell you. I really haven't seen him since that day."

"Alright, I will be in touch if I need anymore information."

"Please do, because this doctor has to go down." He says while checking his clip on his 45. He has a gun because he a medical doctor in a low income, high crime area but now he sees that he can use it for other reasons.

"Yeah, I know. I promise you that he will." He said with confidence.

After the doctor hangs up the phone, he peeks through the gun's sight and points it at a book case. *"If I only had the chance."* He thought to himself.

The nurse hangs up the phone and puts her head down and sighs. "The saga continues." she added with her sigh.

That Boy Got to Go

Meanwhile, back at the Johnson's, Fred comes home from being in the streets all day. When he arrived home, he waste no time calling Brent who he has been trying to reach for sometime now. He hasn't been picking up his phone at all. So he calls Russ to see where Brent was.

"Hello Russ. Have you seen or heard from Brent?" Fred asked him as soon as he answers the phone.

"Don't act like you don't know."

"Know what?"

"You know about Brent's brother, right?"

"No. I never met him?"

"Boy he's dead! Aye Brent didn't call you to set me up did he."

"What! What happened?" responded Fred with a dropped jaw.

"Man is you for real?" he asked curiously. "Boy it is around town and on the news and stuff about a man got shot at a grocery store after an attempted robbery."

"Ah yeah, that was his brother?"

"Ah man I should have told you. My bad."

Silence as Fred takes in the news.

"Man, I don't think he cares to hear from me but you can give him a call." Russ said while thinking about how he shot his brother by mistake.

"Oh, I been trying but why you think he don't want to hear from you too?"

"Man, you sure are asking a lot of dumb questions! Dude just lost his brother, what else." said Russ as he wants to disconnect the phone call. "Anyway, here, just do this. Call Brent back and leave a message about his brother."

Right at that moment, Mr. Johnson comes walking in. Fred sees him from the corner of his eyes.

"Man it's something else I want to share with you but I can't say it now." Fred said turning around so that he don't have to make eye contact with Mr. Johnson.

Mr. Johnson hears the last of that conversation, looks and starts wondering who Fred was talking too.

"Alright, I have to go." Fred quickly hangs up the phone and turns to walk the opposite way of Mr. Johnson.

"So, Fred who were you talking to, son?" Mr. Johnson asked quickly before Fred enters his room.

"Nobody." Fred replied as he enters his room and closes the door behind him.

He walks over and peeks at the caller ID and realizes nobody tried to call. Then he picks up the receiver and hits redial. *This is my house.* He thought.

"Hey Fred you can talk now?" Russ asked as soon as he answered the phone.

Fred being curious comes out and stands in the doorway wondering if Mr. Johnson was doing what he thinks he was doing.

"Who is this?" asked Mr. Johnson with an uneasy feeling.

"Who is this?" Russ returned.

"This is Mr. Johnson and you are talking to my boy, in my house, and I want to know whose he's talking too!"

"Man, that's not my problem."

"What? I will take this........." He bites his lip.

"What, you will take what? Man get off my phone!" Russ shot back as he disconnect from him.

"Hello, hello." Mr. Johnson being angry realizes that he got hung up on. He turns and sees Fred who is slowly motioning his head without making a face.

"That boy got to go." Mr. Johnson mumbles under his breath. He looks back at Fred with the same expression.

Shortly there after, Mrs. Johnson walks in the room and notices Mr. Johnson's angry face.

"Boy, what's wrong with you?"

Mr. Johnson gives Mrs. Johnson a quick look. "I really think we should let Fred go back to the home. I mean he's talking to strange guys on our phone and I don't feel safe." He pauses with an intense stare in her eyes. "For you or for me." He added.

"Honey we talked about this before and I told you he has already been through a lot, so just wait and stop talking about that before he overhears you. Mrs. Johnson said walking on the other side of the room looking for signs of Fred. "Where is he?" she continued, seeing no signs of Fred.

"I don't know, he was just standing right there." He replied as he points in the direction Fred was standing.

"Boy, what have you done?" she asked looking up at him then down. "He must be mad because he left his favorite red jacket here." She said while bending down and picking up his jacket off from the floor. "He never left without his favorite jacket. You guys really need to mend things."

Mr. Johnson motions his head in disgust that Mrs. Johnson really wants to keep this boy. "Honey is there somewhere I can take you? I think I need to have a man to man talk with Fred."

"I don't know. I guess you can take me to Mrs. Byrd's house. She needs to know that we are really still there, even after her son's funeral."

"Alright, grab your things, so I can get back here with Fred."

"Alright, let me call her." She said walking towards the phone.

"Hello, Fred I was just getting ready to call you." Brent said thinking it was Fred when the caller ID read Johnson's Residents.

"This not Fred. What you getting ready to call him for?" asked Mrs. Johnson.

Mr. Johnson overhears her statement and extends his arm and whispers to Mrs. Johnson to give him the phone.

"My boy hasn't been the same since he left you!" He angrily said into the receiver. "What have you shared with him?" Mr. Johnson asked a second question.

"I didn't say nothing about you killing his father." Brent replied sarcastically.

"Boy I didn't kill his dad; the doctor did. But Fred has been talking to guys I don't even know on my phone. I need to know what did you tell him or if he got something up his sleeves."

"I don't know, but that grown ass man he was talking too is probably the man I need to see. He killed my brother!" Brent said with growing dismay.

"What! He's talking to criminals?" Mr. Johnson replied looking up at Mrs. Johnson who was standing beside him.

"Hey, the next time you catch Fred talking to that grown as man; tell him his life is over just like my brother. Hell, tell the doctor too, I know you talk to him, right."

"Hey Brent, leave the doctor alone, I mean it! It seems like once you get something started with the doctor it never ends."

"But if it wasn't for him and his plans, my brother would still be alive."

"I don't know about that. All I know is making any plans with him is like making a deal with the devil."

"Well I kind of understand why you did that to that man."

"Brent, I have to go, ask your mother is it alright if I bring my wife over to keep her company for a few hours." he quickly said to avoid that topic.

"Y'all just come over everybody else has. And I been like a slave to my mother for these couple of days."

"Yeah, I know about being a slave trying to keep someone happy." Mr. Johnson mumbles as Mrs. Johnson had just walked away to get her things.

"Well, I am trying to keep my mother happy. But again, tell your wife to come on through. I don't think she will mind. Right at that moment, his cell phone vibrates. He looks and sees it's a pay phone. *"Hell I haven't got a pay phone call since I was selling drugs."* he thought.

"Ok, sorry about your brother, alright." Mr. Johnson said suddenly realizing he didn't show his respect.

"Oh yeah thanks and don't worry about me telling because I thought about the situation and I asked myself, what would I have done if I was in that same situation. "Yeah, it was messed up, but I understand. But what's messed up is how you all got his son after killing his daddy. That's not right at all."

"Don't let my wife hear you say that."

"What you say about a wife?" Mrs. Johnson replied who is waiting at the door with her jacket folded in her arms.

Mr. Johnson puts his free hand over the receiver. "I didn't say anything about a wife. Are you ready?" He asked.

She nods.

"Here I come." he said back into the phone.

"Ok, I will see you when you get here." Brent said while quickly grabbing his phone to answer it because the same number just called back.

"Yeah."

"This Fred, Brent. I heard about your brother and I am sorry."

"Oh, thanks man. I just got off the phone with your pops."

"For what? What's going on?" Fred asked wondering if they were looking for him.

"I don't know. He said he's getting ready to drop his wife off over here."

"Oh cool, I got to go. Bye." Fred said quickly as he hangs up and runs back to the house.

"I wonder what he got going?" Brent thought while hanging up the phone and walking back to Ms. Byrd to inform her of the Johnson's comings.

Fred runs back to the house. He gets to the house and Mr. and Mrs. Johnson had already left.

"Cool." He said while running to the back window that he always leaves open.

"He gets in and grabs his back pack and stuffs some clothes and other items in for a comfortable get away. He then goes to Mr. and Mrs. Johnson's bedrooms to steal some money. He checks everywhere and finds some dollars rolled up in one of the nightstands.

"This is better than nothing." he said to himself rolling the dollars back up and putting it in his pocket. He then rushes to the phone and calls Russ. "Can you come get me?" Fred asked as soon as someone picked up the phone.

"What?'

"Russ."

"Oh it's you this time. I thought you were that man again. I was getting ready to curse him out. But what you mean, come get you?"

"I just wanna leave here and I mean for good."

"But ain't your dad rich?" he asked.

"Russ, can you meet me at Barry's Warehouse and Supplies?" Fred asked without responding to his question.

"Yeah, I know where that is. Give me a half an hour. Where are you trying to go?"

"I am just trying to get the hell away from here."

"Ah man what happened? Did that man hit you?"

"No, not yet. I think he knows I know about what he did to my father and he probably knows that that bullet that killed Ted was supposed to be for him."

"Yeah, that can be a lot of pressure." There is silence as he thinks of the pressure Fred may be going through.

"You know where you going to live?"

"I don't know."

"Oh, so we are running without a plan. I tell you what; you can stay with me and my peeps. I stay in the basement and they will never know you staying with me. I can teach you the game one on one, bet. I will see you in thirty minutes. Oh, don't tell nobody where you going to be, not even Brent. Hell, I don't need kidnapping on my record too."

"Alright." Fred replied while quickly hanging up the phone and climbing back out the window he came in.

"Ah man," he forgot to leave Mrs. Johnson a letter. "I will just call." he said to himself.

Meanwhile, Mr. Johnson gets back home and there is still no sign of Fred. He throws his keys on the table and looks on a telephone list that Mrs. Johnson made for important numbers. He finds the number he was looking for and dials it.

"Hello this is Mr. Wally." someone answered when Mr. Johnson called.

"Hello, Mr. Wally. How have you been?"

"Fine, thanks for asking. Who am I speaking with?"

"This is Mr. Johnson."

"Mr. Johnson... Mr. Johnson." he said twice trying to place his name.

"Uh Fred." Mr. Johnson said to offer a hint.

"Oh yeah, now I remember. Hey, sorry for that memory loss, but what's up? How is the boy doing? Well, young man, I probably should say. How old is he now about 13 or 14?"

"Yeah, I guess. But have you heard what he's been through." He asked quickly to get right to the reason he called.

"No not really. He hasn't had any brush ends with the law, has he?"

"Has he?"

"Oh, we probably won't get that information unless it's a court order. We are dealing with a juvenile." A brief pause. "Is there something you need to share with me?"

"Yeah, I don't think it's working out with Fred."

"What? You had him for all four years and you just now came to this conclusion."

"Well, I haven't been here for some of those years."

"Oh yeah that's right, because Mrs. Johnson ended up adopting him herself. You know what? I mean to tell you the truth; since she was still married at the time of the adoption I still needed your signature. But I just let the adoption go through because she made a promise that everything was alright. It was important for me to see the child get a home. So I wrote a note on there that he is still a ward of the state until we get your signature. Therefore, it might be real easy to give him back because he still will be considered a ward of the state."

"Well cool, this is one signature that I am not mad is missing." he said under his breath thinking about his marriage certificate. "But, I will let you know what we are going to do. Me and Fred are supposed to have a man to man talk whenever he gets here."

"Good, I hope you'll work things out. You know I still remember that day vividly when you guys said that you were going to adopt Fred. He was walking around here in his little red jacket like he was the baddest thing on earth with his new strong dad and all."

"O yeah." he said hearing a beep.

"Hey, how is Mrs. Johnson doing?"

"She's alright. But I got to go. I have another call coming in."

"Oh, alright. Tell her I said hi. And again I hope you all work things out."

"Alright, I will be in touch." replied Mr. Johnson while reading the caller ID for the incoming call. It read private.

"Hello." he answered anyway.

"Hello, where is Mrs. Johnson?" Fred asked in a tone as if he didn't care to talk to Mr. Johnson.

"Boy, where are you and whose phone you on?" Mr. Johnson asked anxiously ready to have his man to man talk.

"Oh yeah, that's right." He thought about what Brent told him earlier about who was coming to his house for his mother. "Never mind."

He hangs up on him and calls Brent's cell phone again.

"Yeah?" Brent answers.

"Brent."

"Yeah, is this little Fred, what's up? Where are you?"

"Nothing. Are you still over to your mom's house?"

"No, I left right after your pops left from over there."

"Well, can I have the number? I have to talk to my mother."

"Alright." A brief pause. Hey, I tell you what. Let me just call her on three-way, I will put down the phone so you all can talk privately."

Brent did exactly that and when he finished dialing the number and Mrs. Byrd answers it.

"Hello."

"Hello mama are you still doing ok?"

"Yeah, I am doing my best, what's up?"

"Can you put Mrs. Johnson on the phone. Fred wants to speak to her."

"I knew you knew where he was, hold on." Ms. Byrd said while giving Mrs. Johnson the phone.

Brent made an attempt to tell her what's going on but Ms. Byrd had already release the phone to Mrs. Johnson.

Mrs. Johnson quickly takes the phone and puts it to her ear.

"Hello." she answered in a questionable tone.

"Hello. Mother, I am running away from home and it has nothing to do with you, but with your husband. Why did you let him come back? We were doing find without him, don't you think?"

Silence.

"Hello?" Fred asked after noticing the silence.

"Son, where are you? Are you with Ms. Byrd's son?" she asked refusing to tackle that question.

"No I am not with him. I am running away. I don't want to stay with you people anymore. Good bye!" Fred disconnect the phone and rides silently on the way to Russ's apartment. When they get to the house, Russ gets out the car first and Fred stays sitting in the passenger seat sitting and staring as he was in a daze. Russ then looks inside the car.

"A man what are you going to do about school?" he asked.

"I hate that nerdy school anyway. I am not going back."

"Well, you know I dropped out early and school ain't done nothing for me but waste my time." He continued to look at Fred inside the door frame and Fred looks at him back and gives him a nod. "Come on, I will show you how to live out here in the streets and make some real money."

Fred exited the car and walks towards the apartment.

Let Me Live

Brent's mother calls the phone back after Fred's and Mrs. Johnson's disconnection.

"Boy, you got her son?"

She didn't bother to let him answer before she spoke again.

"Look here Brent you need to bring her son back here. I know you don't want kidnapping on your record now. Come on… Do the right thing. You are all I got now." She added still not giving Brent a chance to speak.

"But"… Brent tried to get out that he wasn't with Fred but Ms. Byrd doesn't let him get a word out.

"But nothing, Brent don't come back without him. And that's final! I knew you were still the same!" She hangs up on Brent.

"Now where can he be?" He thought to himself. He lets out some air and calls Russ. The phone rings four times and Brent just hangs up. He pressed redial.

"Alright, this is Brent. Don't say a word." Russ told Fred.

"So you finally decided to come around that it was just a mistake, huh. _____ "Hello, hello. Russ said twice after realizing that the phone has been disconnected. He presses the call back button.

"So, you decided to come around and see that it was a mistake, huh." asked Russ again when he heard Brent pick up the line.

"Killing my brother is no mistake man. But first Fred is missing, have you heard from him. My mom's is tripping and thinks I got something to do with him missing. I can't have her mad at me now."

Silence as Russ contemplates to tell him or not.

"Man, I am going to need all my money. It wasn't nothing in those bags but some tapes." Russ said bodly.

"Oh that's why he came back." Brent mumbled to himself. The phone was silent as he briefly thinks of that day. Anger raise as he answers. "Russ do you actually think I am going to pay you for that fuck up."

"Man, I didn't know that was your brother. You gave me specific directions and I did that."

"You probably would had thought smarter if you won't high."

"Man have my money or."

"Or what?"

Russ walks further into the yard to make sure Fred don't hear him.

"Or you won't get Fred back." He said boldly.

"Oh ok. So you do have him. Now where is he?" he asked with determination.

"What?"

"Man, You heard me. Is he with you now?" Brent asked again in a demanding tone.

Russ walks towards the house.

"Hey, if anything happens to Fred, you are still mines two times." He said using the same demanding tone, this time throwing two fingers in the air.

"So, I guess it don't matter huh?"

"You guess what don't matter?"

Russ walks away from the house again.

"Again, if you want to see Fred again, let me live."

A brief pause. As anger builds up inside of him. "Where is Fred man?"

"He is here with me." Russ answers walking back into his apartment.

"Boy, my momma is going to kill me if you don't get Fred back here now."

"Well Fred don't want to go back to them now. He said he didn't want to stay with that man no more."

"Man I should have kept my mouth shut and kept the promise when the doctor had shared that story with me." Brent thought to himself.

"Are y'all at your place? I can be there in a second."

"Hey Fred, you still can change your mind now. Because, that was Brent and he said that he was on his way to get you. So are you sure you don't want to go back." He asked again knowing that he's about to take a dash for it and he's not so sure if he's going to return.

Fred nods expressionless.

"Alright, we got to roll then, before he gets here. I don't want to look at him now either."

Fred and Russ runs out of the back door and into the car.

"So, are you ready to go so I can show you how to run these streets and make a man out of you?" Russ asked Fred turning the key in the ignition.

"Yeah, that's cool." replied Fred as he turns his head helping Russ look for oncoming traffic.

"Now remember if we run into Brent, run because if you don't, he is going to send you back to that man and I know you don't want to go back there." he said as he puts the car in drive and drives into the street.

Fred nods.

They hit the streets and Russ told him everything he learned from Ted and Brent. He also shared with him everything he learned on his own.

Can We Meet II

The doctor continues to look for Brent. Not to see how he's doing but to work on his next plan. Sitting in a hotel lobby, he finally gets a call from Brent.

"Hello, boy where have you been?" asked the doctor as he was sure it was him.

"Excuse me, but my damn brother is dead! I guess that don't matter to you, right."

"Yeah, I heard. Did the cops kill him or did he get caught in some cross fire between the two of you?"

"Doctor you know how my brother died. Why are you trying to be stupid?"

"What?" "I won't there."

"Man, whatever! You don't care. All you care about is killing the detective." Brent said as he bites his lip.

"Yeah, speaking of the detective I got another plan."

"What!" Brent suddenly thinks about the money he needs to get from the doctor. He bites his lip again. Like Russ, Brent thought he will be facitious by asking for the rest of his money. "Can I just get the rest of my money?"

"Brent, do you want to hear the plan or what? You know you don't get no more money until the job is completely done."

"Lets just meet somewhere and we can talk about this plan later." Brent said not sure if he was ready to get the doctor just now. He will rather wait until this recent incident calms down. So his brother's death won't be connected to him.

"Well… "I guess you can meet me up here at the hotel?"

"Well, how about in a couple of hours?" He asked hoping that the detective can finish this up.

"Alright, then call me back when you are on your way." The doctor said to hurry up the process. "In the meantime, I will be working on the plan."

"Alright, good-bye."

He also thinks about the promise he made with the detective and their deal. So he calls up the detective.

"Hello Detective Mac."

"Detective."

"Uh, Brent is this you. What's wrong with you now?" asked the detective feeling Brent's anger through the phone.

"Nothing   man.   What's   up?"
"Why, you say that? What's going on?"

"Well, I just talked to the doctor."

The detective completely stopped what he was doing and starts paying more attention to him.

"OK, what's happening?" he asked in a calm voice.

"Well he wants to meet again for another plan to kill you."

"What. He just won't give up will he? Well, where you guys going to meet?"

"At Barry's Suite's."

"OK, so that's where he's staying at, huh?

"Yeah, I guess."

"You mind wearing a wire. Naw, never mind that. He may be prepared for that since we did that to him last time. A brief moment of silence. "I got an idea. Do you know which room he's in?"

"Naw, man. I was going to call him when I get there."

"When do you suppose to be going?" the detective asked.

"In a couple of hours."

"What? Well we are going to have to hurry. I will get one of my female officers to dress as a house keeper and go in his room and plant one of our digital recorders in his room.

"Alright man whatever."

"I will be talking to you soon. Let me go and grab that cop."

I'm Getting Ready to Call the Doctor

Mr. Johnson is picking up his wife who is furious about what Fred said and doing. "Oh no, why the mean mug?" Mr. Johnson said when he walked in and saw Mrs. Johnson sitting in the front room by the lamp with her arms cross."Did you tell him? I told you that I wanted to be with you if we ever decided to tell him something like that." said Mrs. Johnson with a plain face expression and mean stare.

"Wait a minute, what are you talking about?" he replied with a hard stare back at her.

"You know, about us being involved with the killing of his dad."

"Baby, I never told that boy nothing like that. Who do you take me for?"

"Well, somebody told him and I am not happy about it."

"I know." Mr. Johnson returned nodding his head showing his understanding.

"Well Fred was not at home and he never returned but he did call to speak to you. You think the reason he is acting so off the wall is because he may have found out what we had did to his dad."

"I mean, I will be too." Ms. Byrd said out loud over hearing them.

Mr. Johnson and Mrs. Johnson both look at her to say they thought that this was a private conversation.

"Oh, excuse me I forgot I was in my house." She said looking around. "I will just go in my room to let you guys talk alone and let me just say if there was an opportunity to save my son like y'all tried to save your son, only God knows what I would had done. But you should just let God handle the situation."

"Did you tell her?" Mr. Johnson whispered to Mrs. Johnson when she turned around.

"I had to tell somebody, you won't here to talk to me, remember you left." She whispered back.

Mr. Johnson just motions his head expressionless.

"No Mrs. Byrd you don't have to go to your room. You right this is your house. We can finish talking in the car. And give me a call if you talk to your son when he calls back with Fred."

"What, my son got Fred. I will." then he thought to have Brent get rid of Fred just remembering what kind of work he does. "No, I can't do that." He said out loud by mistake.

"What?" The two ladies said at the same time.

"Never mind that. Where is your phone? I left my cell phone in the car."

"In the kitchen." said Ms. Byrd pointing in the direction of the kitchen.

"Alright." Mr. Johnson took a couple of steps and Mrs. Johnson stops him.

R. D. SIMMONS

"Hold on, I don't know who you are getting ready to call but I am seeing a longer conversation than expected. So let's not worry Ms. Byrd with our problems anymore and go get your cell from the car."

Mrs. Johnson gets up and took some copy steps behind Mr. Johnson who turns around to head out the door.

"Honey, can you just wait in the house? I will come and get you when I am through." He asked as he stops the stride suddenly.

She broke her stride as well preventing herself from bumping into him.

"What you mean? Fred is my son too."

"I am getting ready to call the doctor." Mr. Johnson said tilting his head to the right and raising a brow.

"Alright, I am already mad. No senses in letting the doctor get me madder."

"Good, I will be right back."

Mr. Johnson calls the doctor and gets an answering service.

He hangs up and calls right back.

"Hello."

"Hello, doctor what's Brent's number?"

"Hold on." A brief pause. "Alright, so what's up? Why do you need his number?"

"Well he supposed to be with my son."

175

"How is that? I just talked to him not to long ago."

"He didn't say nothing about Fred?" No all he was talking about was that dead brother of his. By the way, I got another plan."

"Doc, I am sure Brent is like me. We had enough of your damn plans."

"This will definitely work. It got too."

"You right it got too. But if it don't, will you still leave me alone."

"I will try. Now remember we are here because what you had me to do for your son."

A moment of silence as Mr. Johnson closes his eyes and lets out some anger.

"Alright, I deserve that."

"I know you deserve that! What you say back then? Doctor, I will be there for you. I give you my word. Then we shook on it."

"Doc, it's not like you needed me anymore. It's not my fault that you trust thugs."

"How can you say that? You didn't know what I needed. You were only worried about you."

"Well anyway, I am a little worried now. I am almost sure if we don't find Fred, my wife is going to blame his missing on me. Hell, I still think she have some heartfelt feeling that I had something to do with my son's death. So I defiantly don't care to add this one on there."

"We are not going to that saga again. Now you need Brent's number because you say he got your son, Fred." He said before putting him on speaker phone and going through his numbers on his phone.

"Yeah so what's his number?"

"I tell you what; I will put the two of you on three way because I need to talk to him anyway."

"Alright, I'll hold." Mr. Johnson said not even thinking about questioning why he needed to do that.

The phone rings and Brent answers the phone realizing it's the doctor as he looks at his caller id.

"Hey doc, I should be there in 30 minute."

"Okay. I am in suite 214. Just come up."

"Alright."

"Yeah."

"Well Mr. Johnson needs to ask you something. Mr. Johnson, are you still there? No answer. "Mr. Johnson." he called his name again. "Well I guess he hung up."

"Oh, you had him ease dropping, huh?" Brent said on the other end with one wide eye.

"No, he was trying to reach you because he says you got his son."

"I don't have his son. Hell my mother doesn't want to hear from me because she thinks I got his son too. Man, there is a lot of confusion with this."

"Whatever. Hold on, somebody is trying to get in my room."

"Housekeeping." Said the worker as she opens the door.

"Huh? Excuse you. Did my Do Not Disturb sign fall down or something?" He asked wondering what made this housekeeper to just walk-in. "Brent, I will see you when you get her. I got to call somebody about this rudeness.

Like A Pro

Meanwhile, Russ and Fred are just pulling up to the hotel.

"You can stay here?" Fred asked when he stopped the car. "Yeah, it's a first. Come on nobody will ever expect us to be here."

Fred nods in amazement.

Fred and Russ checked in their room and they really like what they saw.

"Yeah baby, this is nice." Russ said as he walks further inside the hotel room.

Fred agrees again as he takes quick steps to grab the remote and sit down on the sofa.

"Alright, cuz don't get too comfortable, we only going to be here for a day or two. I got to figure out my next move. Since you are going to be my road dawg, I need to give you something. Hold up let me put this in the bedroom.

Meanwhile, Brent walks in the hotel were the doctor is in. He by passes the reception desk as he knows what room to go too. He enters the elevator after the door opens and a housekeeper walks out of it.

"Detective, this is Officer Wright. The bug is planted behind a bottle of Brandy dark. Tell your boy."

"Good, job. Alright let me call him." He said as he quickly disconnects the phone knowing that Brent was on his way there. The hotel provided poor reception and therefore the call didn't get through. He calls the officer back. "So what happened? Did he give you a hard time?"

"He was giving me a hard time at first but when I told him that I was here to restock the bar, he calmed down." She answered him glad to tell him her brave story.

Meanwhile, upstairs from her the elevator door opens up for Brent to exit. Brent steps out and looks at the wall and notices the numbers on it telling him which way to go.

Just after the elevator door close, Mr. Johnson walks in the hotel lobby looking for Fred. He walks to the reception counter.

As soon as he gets to the counter, he is greeted by the receptionist. He quickly asked for what he needs.

"Have you seen a boy with another young man in here?"

"Yeah, I guess. But who are you? Are they expecting you?"

"Oh so he's here already huh? Man I knew he had my son." he mumbles to himself.

The phone rings at the front desk. The receptionist picks up the phone, holding one finger in the air asking Mr. Johnson to excuse him.

"Front desk." He answered.

"Man it's only one bed in our room." The other caller replied in an angry tone.

"What room you calling from 240? He answered his own question looking at the switchboard. "Owe you just came in with that little boy huh. Okay sorry about that you want to change that."

"Yeah."

"As a matter of fact," he looks up and notices Mr. Johnson is already headed to the elevator.

"Sir!" He yelled, trying to get his attention.

Mr. Johnson turns around taking back steps towards the elevator. He puts and okay sign up to inform the receptionist he doesn't need his help no more.

"The receptionist informs Russ to what is happening.

"Is somebody looking for you?"

"Somebody like who?"

"Well some guy just came up here looking for you and I think he may have put two and two together when I called out your room number out loud by mistake. So I think he's on his way up there. You need me to call security?"

"Yeah do that." Russ hangs up the phone quickly and turns to Fred. "Fred did you tell Brent we was here?"

"No. What's going on?" he asked.

Russ runs to the room and to a bag. Before he grabs what's in it, the phone rings. He drags the bag to the phone with him and answers it.

"Hello." He answered attaching the phone to his ear and shoulders as he searches threw a bag.

"Aye security got your man and they are bringing him back down now." The front counter receptionist informed him so you don't have to worry now.

"Man good. Is he going to jail? Well we can only make him leave the premises for now. But if he tries to get back in, we will stop him and then we may arrest him for trespassing."

"Good, we may need another room ASAP. Thanks to you he knows where I am now."

"Well, the hotel is booked. You took the last room we had." He said checking the rooms on the computer. "I will be sending you another bed there in a minute."

"Man, alright." He sighs, as he looks in his hand at the gun he just took out of the bag. He glances up at Fred.

In the meantime, Mr. Johnson is just getting escorted out of the hotel's front lobby doors. As soon as he was outside, he swiftly lifts his arm away from the security guards grip.

"Man don't come back in here today or we are going to have to arrest you for trespassing." The security guard told Mr. Johnson throwing him out.

At the same time, the doctor is laying another plan on Brent. He doesn't realize that Brent is trying to set him up.

"Now do you see how this going to work?" asked the doctor talking to Brent.

"Yeah. But can you make me a drink and tell me again?"

"So now I am your maid huh?

Brent smirks.

"You know what? Because your brother had died, I guess you need this drink, huh." He replies from his smirky expression as he gets up and heads towards the bar. "Now I got to tell you, I am not giving you any of this white liquor at the bar. So all you get is the dark liquor, so is Brandy ok." He asked as he's reaching for the bottle.

This is for Our Proctection II

Russ hangs up the phone from talking to the front desk. He walks towards Fred with a gun in his hand.

"Fred, have you ever shot one of theses." Russ asked when he got in front of him.

Fred never responds and just looks at the pistol in his hand.

"But I hope you held one before right?"

"Yeah." He replies remembering the day when Ted caught him with that gun.

"Here, this is for our protection." He said handing Fred the pistol but never releasing it to give it to him.

He nods as that day when Ted died became more vividly.

"So now it's me and you. I got your back and you got my back alright. We don't need anybody trying to separate us alright; we got an agreement or a promise."

Fred just stands there glancing back and forth at him and the gun in his hand and Russ.

"So, you ever killed someone before?"

Fred quickly lifts his eye brow to get Russ' attention.

"O, my bad. I forgot. So I guess I am not talking to a rookie huh?"

Fred lifts his shoulders up and down.

"So, again this is for our protection, I got your back, you got my back, bet."

Fred nods. As that day of Ted telling him that pops in his head.

"Yah, so if that man come or Brent come, be ready to use it."

"Brent?" Fred questioned.

"He told me he's trying to get you too, so you can go back and stay with that man you know that you don't like. So you see, I am doing you a favor. How many other friends will do something like this for you? How many?"

"Okay cool." Fred spoke softly.

"Man you are a cool little boy. You good people. Fred man I am going to tell you about my first time killing someone, and it wasn't with a gun." He said releasing the gun and turning his back to Fred to put away his things.

As he tells Fred about his first killing, Mr. Johnson is walking back and forth on the sidewalk as he was unable to get the hotel security to summit to his request. He stops his pace and reaches in his pocket to call the doctor. He puts the phone to his ear after dialing his number.

"Doctor. I need your help." Mr. Johnson spoke into the phone.

"I thought this day will come back around. What is it this time?"

"Well I think Fred is in your hotel."

"Yeah, what make you think that?"

"I got a hint from the hotel clerk."

"Well he's not with Brent. Brent is here with me alone drinking up my white liquor. Talking about the dark liquor makes him sick. I thought all y'all like dark liquor." He said jokingly.

"Well I need a favor because I still got a hunch that he is in your hotel." He asked as he quickly glances up the hotel building not acknowledging his bold yet bias comment.

"Doctor, who's asking about me?" Brent asked in the background.

"This Mr. Johnson." he quickly whispers to him.

"He got Fred?" asked Brent excitedly in the background again.

"Well the front desk told me that an older teenager and a younger teenager had just check in and I am not leaving her until I find out who is in that room." said Mr. Johnson with determination.

"What room?" asked the doctor as he puts one finger in the air for Brent to wait on an answer. "What room you talking about Mr. Johnson?"

"Room 240 is what the front desk said."

"O, is that right. You got that information from the front desk hotel?"

"I overheard a conversation over the phone that sounds like it will be them in that room."

"Alright, I tell you what, I will have Brent to check the room to see if he's in there."

"Where is he at?" Brent asked anxiously in the background again.

"He thinks he is in room 240." The doctor tells Brent and he quickly walks out the hotel room headed to room 240.

As the doctor was telling him what room he thinks Fred was in, a lady wearing a housekeeping dress had just approach Mr. Johnson.

"Sir it may be kind of dangerous here because something may go down here soon." The lady tells him showing him her police badge.

He nods at the officer.

"What's going on Mr. Johnson?" asked the doctor.

"I don't know, some cop just walked up to me dress up like a housekeeper telling me that something is about to go down here."

The doctor looks at the bar. "Hold on or just let me call you back." He said hanging up the phone and walking slowly to the bar. He slides some bottles to the side and what do you know, he sees the recorder behind the dark Brandy. "I will be damn." He shouted as he motions his head. He grew furious from what he saw. He picks the tape recorder up and walks to the restroom and flushes it down the toilet. He walks slowly towards the nightstand where he was keeping his gun. After checking his clip, he walks out his hotel room headed to room 240 to get Brent.

As Mr. Johnson was getting to walk to his car, he noticed a customer come out of the secured door. "Hey, hey don't close that door. I left my key in my room." He runs to the door as the man kindly held it open for him.

As Brent is walking to get to Fred, Mr. Johnson and the doctor are on their way to the same place. At the same time, Russ is just now finishing up telling Fred what had happen when he first killed someone.

"Fred man it was wild. Cause my friends were joking me, talking about why I stop a man from getting his last meal, because the news said that they found some coupons to McDonald's and a movie in his pocket. I guess he will never get that meal or see that movie, now huh." he smiles as he turns from putting stuff away. Feeling Fred looking at him, he turns and sees him nervously pointing the gun directly at him.

Russ' smile slowly evaporates as he sees irritation in Fred's eyes as they fills up with water.

"That was my daddy... He was going to take me to McDonalds and the movies."

The End